About the Author

Maria is a minister's wife living in northwest England and is actively involved in her local church and wider Christian organisations. She has always loved writing and also enjoys swimming, walking, spending time with friends and a good cup of coffee.

Merry
Christmas
Luc!

Lots of
love
Jo :)
xxx

Lottie's Locket

Maria Johnson

Lottie's Locket

Olympia Publishers
London

www.olympiapublishers.com
OLYMPIA PAPERBACK EDITION

A CIP catalogue record for this title is
available from the British Library.

ISBN: 978-1-78830-797-0

First Published in 2020

Olympia Publishers
Tallis House
2 Tallis Street
London
EC4Y 0AB

Printed in Great Britain

Dedication

For my two lovely goddaughters, Evie-Beth and Mikaela.
May they have an adventure when reading this book.

"I will sing the wondrous story
Of the Christ who died for me,
How He left His home in glory
For the cross of Calvary."

Part One

Chapter One

"Come on, Lottie! You really need to get up now, we're going to be late!"

Lottie scowled resolutely at the white, speckled ceiling above her. The ten-year-old girl stubbornly bit her lip. It was a strong act of defiance not to leave her bed. Her cause was made even stronger by how deliciously snug her duvet was wrapped around her. How could anyone expect her to leave such a wonderful cocoon of comfort?

"Come on, Lottie!" The stressed call of her mother came again, clearly annoyed. Lottie sighed. She knew how unrealistic it would be that she got her own way. Her parents were hardly likely to drive off without her, leaving her to spend the whole day in bed.

The mature part of Lottie (for, of course, she was only a few days away from becoming eleven) knew that one way or the other, she would have to go to her Aunt Susan's house today. All she had to do was decide whether she would go quietly, or after a massive row with her parents.

"Coming, Mum," Lottie eventually called downstairs, trying and failing miserably to keep the utter resignation from her voice. As much as she wanted to stay at home while her parents went swanning off to visit her sister Nadia in Newcastle, falling out with them wouldn't do anyone any good. So it was that she reluctantly left the cocoon of comfort, moving to sit up in bed. Though it was the Easter holidays and they were well into April, Lottie shivered, still feeling a chill to the morning air.

Lottie ran a hand through her wavy hair that stopped just below her shoulders, looking around her bedroom. Her bed was positioned neatly in the corner of her bedroom, with most of it just below her big window to her right. The curtains were still drawn, but enough light filtered through to let her know the day was going to be sunny.

There were the three wide shelves opposite her, containing all her books. It really was all of them, too—even now, she could see the colouring books and the small ones with the flaps she'd played with when she was little. Her mum kept nagging her to get rid of them, but for now Lottie had won the battle to keep them and they sat there proudly, clean lines smudged by crayons.

Next to her bookshelves was the small desk where she did her homework and played games on the laptop, currently switched off. On the desk chair, currently wheeled round to face her, were the clothes she'd left out the night before. Square in the middle of the carpet was her blue and black suitcase. Lottie scowled at it, knowing it symbolised everything that was wrong this morning.

Looking away from the offensive luggage, she glanced to her immediate left. The wall of her wardrobe faced her, complete with a poster of a boyband she'd once liked. Lottie had moved on to other music years ago but had never bothered to pull it down. Neatly arranged in little rows on top of her wardrobe were all the cuddly animals and teddy bears she'd had when she was younger.

Reluctantly, Lottie leant forward to pull open her curtains, admitting daylight into the previously rather dark and cosily lit room. As her bed aligned right next to the window, the windowsill also acted as her bedside table. She glanced at her alarm clock and her eyes widened. It was getting on for 9; a fair bit later than she'd thought. No wonder her mum was getting stressed.

Seeing how late it was, at last, spurred Lottie into action. She stood and stretched, before grabbing her brush to set about attacking her hair. She smoothed out the rough knots quickly, before tying it back with a hairband into a simple ponytail. Then she got changed, throwing her pyjamas into the case and dressing in the clothes on the desk chair.

"Don't forget to take your toothbrush," came her mother's friendly warning, just as Lottie left her bedroom. Lottie paused on the landing, scowling again. Her mother had already reminded her the night before. Besides, she was hardly likely to forget it. Didn't her mother trust her? Lottie glared further at the frayed carpet at her feet, realising her mum was probably waiting at the foot of the stairs, listening for the sounds of her daughter finally moving. She made sure to stomp to the bathroom, closing the door loudly behind her.

After Lottie brushed her teeth, she held it in her hand a moment. She was tempted to forget it on purpose to spite her mother's nagging—but then she thought of Aunt Susan taking her into the village to get another one, all the while probably telling her off about it. All in all, the rebellion probably wasn't worth the hassle, so she dutifully placed her toothbrush and toothpaste into her light-blue transparent bathroom bag.

The girl headed back into her bedroom much quieter this time, throwing her bathroom bag into the suitcase. Next, Lottie picked up the novel she was halfway through and the puzzle book next to her bed. She'd better not forget her brush, either, throwing that into the suitcase too. Lottie strapped on her watch and glanced round her bedroom a final time, checking she hadn't forgotten anything. Then, there was nothing else to do but seal up her case.

Lottie flipped the lid, then took her time crawling the zip all the way around. It was as if closing her suitcase was her final acceptance, resigning herself to the inevitable fate of staying at her Aunt Susan's creepy old house in rural Yorkshire. Her begrudging agreement to go didn't mean she was in any hurry to get there quicker, though, so Lottie still loitered a few seconds in her room, stewing in all her grumpiness. Eventually, then, Lottie picked up her thin, navy jacket, slung it over her arm and headed downstairs. Her dad would bring down the suitcase later.

"Ah, here we are, at last!" Her mother's relief was palpable. "Cereal's on the table, love," she added brightly, smiling a little too broadly, softening the angle of her cheekbones. Lottie fought not to grimace as she entered the kitchen. It was her mum's overly cheery tone that grated on her. Her mother often used it when she was stressed, but unfortunately, it was also totally patronising and made her feel like a child.

"Morning, Mum, Dad," Lottie greeted, trying to sound neutral as she shook cereal into her bowl. From the way her mother's lips grew tighter together before leaving the kitchen, the girl could tell her voice had still come out sullen.

"I still don't see why I have to stay with Aunt Susan." Lottie's quiet grumble was directed to her father, currently sat opposite her at the table. His arms were stretched wide from reading his broadsheet newspaper, blocking most of his face.

"Why can't I come with you?" Her dad sighed loudly as Lottie reached for her spoon.

"We went over this last night, Lottie." Her dad spoke quietly, but the irritation was clear enough as he folded the newspaper once in half, then once again before placing it on the kitchen table. Now she had a proper view of her father, Lottie noticed the knot in his eyebrows and how there seemed to be bigger circles around his eyes, just visible underneath his glasses. There was also dark stubble gathering on his usually clean face, which wasn't like him at all. Her father's stern face softened a little, then, pushing his glasses further up on his nose before speaking.

"Nadia's not having a great time of it recently," her dad said, his voice now gentle and reasonable. "You know her hairdresser business hasn't been going too well, plus she's been having problems with Sean." Sean was Nadia's boyfriend. Lottie had only met him the once at a family party and hardly knew anything about him. The girl swallowed a mouthful of cereal.

"Yeah, I know, but..." Lottie paused and frowned. "Why do you have to send me off to Aunt Susan's? I'm not a kid anymore, I could handle it." Her dad frowned again, but more in thought than being cross with her.

"It's not about what you might be able to handle, that's not why you're going," her dad sighed. He sat forward a little in his chair, placing his elbows on the table while he watched her a moment. The way he knotted his fingers together under his chin made him look like a detective.

"You think that because we're sending you to Susan's, we're treating you like a child," her dad guessed. Lottie nodded, unable to help from scowling again as she had her last mouthful of cereal. To try to hide it, she lifted the bowl to slurp down the leftover milk.

"Actually, it's quite the opposite," her dad said. If he'd noticed her glare, he didn't comment. "We're actually expecting you to be very grown up." Lottie glanced up at him as she put the bowl back on the table, confused. "Lottie, it's Nadia who is struggling to handle things right now," he explained. "Your mum and I need to focus on helping her."

"But you'll miss my birthday!" Lottie burst out. She knew this really did make her sound like a child, but she couldn't help it. "I only turn eleven once, you know," she grumbled.

"You only turn every year once." Lottie openly rolled her eyes at her dad's attempt at a joke. "All right, I know. We're sorry about that, we really are. I know it sucks," he emphasised. "That's why we're asking you to be grown up." He reached out a hand to pat hers briefly.

"It might surprise you to know we don't particularly want to go either," he admitted. Lottie jerked her head up at his from where she had been scowling again at the table. "Your mum has been very stressed and worried about Nadia, love. She's had to say she can't go into her school this week and I've had to rearrange important meetings at work." Lottie frowned, considering this.

"It's a very adult thing, to have to get on and do things you don't want to do," her dad continued, "to see things from other people's point of view. To see that Nadia needs help at the moment. That's what we're asking you to do, too. We'll try to make it up to you, I promise." He removed his hand.

"So, it would really help," he added, his voice hardening slightly, "if you could try and be a bit less grumpy about it. All right?" Lottie had been turning her cereal spoon over in her hand, but at this she looked up at her father.

"All right," she agreed. Her face was still creased with a frown, but not because she was cross still. She was thinking about what her dad had said. Nadia was twelve years older than her and as such, she hadn't seen her that much over the years. It was so strange to think that Nadia, in her early twenties, might need help and looking after, rather than her the ten-year-old.

"Good girl." Her dad smiled, looking relieved. "I'll go get your case," he added, getting up from the kitchen table, his hand touching her shoulder as he left. Lottie stayed where she was, absently staring at the cereal box still in the middle of the kitchen table.

Lottie had always thought of Nadia as supremely confident and independent. For the first time, the girl wondered what her bossy older sister might really be struggling with. With that she stood to go and rinse her bowl and spoon in the sink and put the milk back in the fridge.

"Nearly ready?" Lottie nodded as her mum came back into the kitchen. "Sit down a minute," she invited, her tone suddenly gentle. The girl did so, starting to feel bad about what a grump she'd been so far today. "I'm sorry we have to miss your birthday, love," Julie Armitage murmured, sadness entering her eyes. "We'll make it really special when we come back. Besides," she added, her tone far brighter, "that doesn't mean you can't have a present to open."

"Thanks, Mum," her daughter smiled, as Julie turned to open her simple brown clasp handbag. She pulled out a thin, long box with purple glittery wrapping paper. Lottie knew it was a bit childish, but she couldn't help the sight of the present and its pretty paper lifting her mood a little.

"This is rather a special present, so I'll get dad to put it in your suitcase to keep it safe for you. You must promise not to open it until your birthday," her mother teased gently.

"All right," Lottie agreed with a grin, intrigued. It would be hard for her not to open such a mysterious present early, but she decided to try her best.

"Come on, then," her mother winked, as they heard her father bringing her suitcase back downstairs. As they entered the hall, her mum unzipped the case a little to slip the present inside. Lottie's mouth turned as her mum and dad left the house ahead of her, a full smile crossing her face for the first time since she'd woken up that morning. For the first time since her parents had told her they were visiting Nadia, Lottie found she was looking forward to her birthday again.

***

Lottie stared out of the window, idly watching the landscape as it rolled by. Presently, she glanced down to check her watch. They were two hours into the journey from the Wirral to her aunt's house, who lived in a village outside of Harrogate. From there, her parents would go on to Newcastle to visit her sister. The girl stretched her arms and sighed, her smile long since gone.

"Nearly there now," her dad commented from the driver's seat as they turned off a main road. Aunt Susan lived in a large converted barn, which sounded so lovely and grand, but Lottie had always hated it as a child. Mostly, she remembered doors that were far too creaky or strange sounds outside at night. Now she was older, Lottie knew the creaking was probably just because the house was old, or that the strange sounds were just owls from the woods nearby. Knowing what the sounds were, though, didn't stop her from feeling anxious about it.

"I'm sure Susan's got lots of exciting things planned for you," Julie commented. Lottie fought not to roll her eyes at her mother, because she knew what 'exciting things' were for Aunt Susan. It meant going around lots of museums and old houses.

Lottie enjoyed museums sometimes, but Aunt Susan had a stuffy way of doing 'tours' to explain what she thought were the most interesting things, which also happened to be some of the least interesting to a ten-year-old girl. The long since dead people who had sat in those chairs or the ancient books in a glass box in the bedroom. Lottie might have been interested in the books if she'd been allowed to look at them properly, but they were kept encased far away, with no one ever allowed to touch them. Lottie knew the books were protected because they were so old, but still, she didn't like the idea of books no longer being read.

"You never know," Malcolm Armitage chimed in. "There's lots of great things to do in the Yorkshire Dales. Sometimes it's like being in another world. You might even have an adventure!"

"Yeah," Lottie murmured, trying not to sound sarcastic, "maybe." She chose not to comment on how Aunt Susan was the least likely person in the world to have adventures. Instead she looked back out of the window, glimpsing the Yorkshire Dales in the distance above the fields and farms around her. Lottie had to admit her dad might be partly right—Aunt Susan might be stuffy, but the rolling fields and hills, the low stone walls and farmhouses that looked years and years old… there was a quiet, gentle beauty about it that did seem another world compared to a bustling city, or even a small town.

"Here we are!" Her mother announced a little needlessly, as the tell-tale click of indicators sounded. It was that same bright, overly enthusiastic tone again that made Lottie feel like she was five. As her dad turned his car into the long, winding drive that led to her aunt's house, Lottie bit her lip, staring at the avenue of trees gracing either side of the path. Despite her best efforts, she could feel her grumpiness seeping back into her veins.

The car crunched and rolled over loose gravel as it pulled to a stop outside her Aunt Susan's house. Her parents got out of the car, with her dad heading for the boot to get her suitcase out. Lottie stayed in her seat a moment longer, before unclipping the seat belt and clambering out herself. Then she stopped and stared at Aunt Susan's house, biting her lip again.

The old barn was as huge and creepy as she'd remembered. Lottie had hoped it would look perfectly ordinary now she was older, but it just didn't. The girl frowned, wondering if Aunt Susan would be as stern as her memories suggested, too.

Lottie didn't need to wait any longer to find that out, for suddenly her mum's sister came striding out of the house, as if conjured by her memory itself. Aunt Susan marched towards them as though she was in the military, with her long dark-grey skirt and crisp white blouse making her look stricter than ever. Her aunt was a few years older than her mother and though her hair looked lighter and peppered with grey and there were a few more lines on her forehead, she hadn't changed much. There was still the neat bob of hair, the pointed nose, the mole on the top of her lip.

"How lovely to see you all!" Susan greeted, a grin suddenly cracking her face and making her look years younger. Lottie watched the two sisters kiss, then she turned to her niece.

"Ah, Lottie, haven't you grown?" Her aunt's eyes crinkled as she smiled in affection, patting her on the shoulder. It reminded her that Susan was as kind as she was prim, which gave her hope.

"Hi, Aunt Susan," Lottie smiled back, trying her best to sound enthusiastic. Her dad turned to lock the car, her suitcase in his free hand. He placed it on the gravel near her feet.

"Come in for a cup of tea," Susan invited, the three adults already making their way towards the house. "Did you have a safe journey?"

"Tea would be great, thanks. Yeah, the traffic wasn't too bad." Her mum stretched her arms a little before letting them drop again to her sides.

Lottie followed, her suitcase wheels clacking against the gravel, glancing to the dense forest surrounding Aunt Susan's house. Turning back to her parents, Lottie caught the subtle glance between her parents, saw the relief flicker in their eyes. They'd obviously thought she'd be grumpy at Aunt Susan, which only made Lottie made annoyed. She scowled at their backs. After all, she might not be overjoyed she was here, but she'd hoped they'd trust her enough not to be rude to the person she was staying with!

"We can't stay very long," her dad was saying as they all trooped inside. "We want to get up to Nadia before the lunchtime rush. You know what city centres can get like." Lottie walked further into the hall, leaving her suitcase near the bottom of the stairs for now. The old wooden floorboards creaked just as much as she remembered. Lottie knew the whole of downstairs was the same—no wonder she remembered it being so creepy!

Also, as clean as Aunt Susan tried to keep the old house, especially because she was so prim and proper, there were still ancient cobwebs hanging in the corners of tall ceilings, where obviously her duster couldn't reach. As Lottie followed her parents and her aunt into the kitchen, she shivered, even though it was mid spring. It seemed like it was as cold in the old barn as she remembered, too.

Standing in the kitchen that was even chillier than the hall, Lottie asked for tea too rather than squash, simply to warm her up a little.

"That's fine, Lottie," said Aunt Susan, looking delighted that her niece had asked for something so grown-up. "Why don't you go on through to the lounge and make yourself at home? We'll be through in a minute with the tea."

"Ok," Lottie agreed, but inside she knew she felt like she was just being told to get out of the way, the way adults did when they wanted to talk about 'serious' things with other adults. Lottie wandered through to the living room, sitting down on a rather uncomfortable sofa. Almost as soon as she'd sat down, Lottie could hear them speaking quickly in low voices, proving her right.

Lottie sighed, guessing her parents were probably talking about Nadia. Though she did feel sorry about her sister's troubles, the girl couldn't help but feel left out, alone in this draughty room whilst her parents and her aunt stayed in the kitchen to talk about her sister. As Lottie shifted on the sofa, feeling it creak under her thighs, the reality sank in that she was here for five days.

"Ah, sorry, Lottie." Her aunt strode into the room, her parents in tow behind her. "We almost forgot about you!" She joked, holding out the tea.

"Thanks," Lottie replied, smiling back, pretending her aunt's words hadn't stung. She caught her mother's eye, seeing sympathy written on her face. Julie Armitage had probably guessed her thoughts—she usually could. Her mum's expression seemed to make everything worse, so she hid her feelings with a quick gulp of tea. The strong, comforting drink swirled in her mouth before slipping gratefully down her throat, warming her insides a little. Lottie wanted to cup her hands around the mug like adults did to fight the chill in her fingers, but it was still too hot.

"So, Lottie," Aunt Susan said after a moment, but then paused. The ten-year-old was awfully aware of the quiet, awkward atmosphere in the room. She could hear every gentle tick of the small clock on the mantlepiece. "Are you still enjoying your swimming?"

"Yes," Lottie answered, then couldn't think of anything else to say. "My teacher said I've improved quite a lot this year."

"You're being far too modest, pumpkin," Malcolm teased, winking at her. "She's nearly the fastest in her year now." Lottie only nodded, internally cringing. She hated bragging or just talking lots about herself. She wasn't overly fond of being spoken about in the third person while she was still in the room, either. The silence lasted a few moments more, before her mother brightly asked Susan something to pick up the conversation.

Extremely glad attention was no longer on her, Lottie roved her eyes around the room, watching the mantlepiece clock. It was one of those with a glass case around it, with a small pendulum that spiralled one way round, then the other.

Lottie listened to their conversation, talking mostly about recent improvements to Aunt Susan's house (including the heating, which Lottie found mildly amusing, given how cold it was) and her job. Her aunt was the manager of a local pub hotel.

"Right, then, we'd better get on the move," Malcolm said at last. With her dad's announcement they all stood and traipsed back outside, where Lottie genuinely thought it was warmer than in the house. The girl found that in a way she was a little relieved her parents were finally going, because she'd found the quiet conversation in the lounge so awkward.

"Bye, Lottie, love," her mum murmured, giving her daughter a big hug that seemed to last a fraction longer than normal. Lottie wondered if her mother didn't really want to go, either.

"Bye, Mum." Lottie sensed her mother's emotion and as she stood back to watch them leave, she found she was suddenly close to tears. As she stood there beside Aunt Susan, raising her hand to wave as they drove away, Lottie felt more miserable than ever. The prospect of having an adventure while she was here had never seemed further away.

Chapter Two

Lottie rolled over in bed, sighing. No matter how she tried, she couldn't get back to sleep. She still couldn't get used to the hardness of her mattress and the scratchiness of the sheets, even after three nights. It couldn't be more different than the cocoon of comfort in her own bed. In the end, Lottie gave up on the idea of sleep for now and sat up, entirely annoyed.

She was now over halfway through her stay in her aunt's house. The house was still not the cosiest, but by now she had gotten used to the slight chill that always seemed to linger in the walls, no matter how many layers she put on. Lottie had been right about 'Aunt Susan's exciting plans', too. It had involved going into various museums in York and Leeds. Whilst some of this had been interesting, soon Lottie had longed for the outdoors and fresh air. They were right next to the Yorkshire Dales, after all!

At least today had been better, the girl reflected. They had gone for a walk in the dales that morning, the spring sunshine both warming her and blowing away the cobwebs. They had ended up in Harrogate itself and as a special treat, Aunt Susan had taken her to the Old Swan Hotel in Harrogate, where the crime writer Agatha Christie had been found after her famously mysterious eleven-day disappearance. Lottie loved Agatha Christie novels and had loved sitting in the elegant dining room, with high ceilings and chandeliers twinkling down at her, wondering if the author had sat at this very table, enjoying finger sandwiches and scones.

Lottie now shivered for the billionth time. She shoved her pillow to a vertical position behind her and sat against it, pressing her covers around her. It had been like this for the last three nights, with Lottie just trying to be warm enough. Aunt Susan had insisted the thick woollen blankets would suffice, but honestly, Lottie didn't think they were much help at all. Sighing again, Lottie reached over to pat the top of her alarm clock. The glaring blue numbers immediately popped up: 12:04. It was officially her birthday.

"Happy birthday to me," Lottie whispered to herself. She thought about lying back down and trying to sleep, but then remembered the special present from her mother. Lottie had managed to resist the temptation to open it—instead, it had remained where it was, tucked in the corner of her suitcase. As it was technically her birthday now, why shouldn't she open it?

With that thought in her mind, Lottie flicked on her bedside lamp and the room was instantly filled with a dim light (Aunt Susan really did need to replace the bulb). She hopped out of bed, flinching a little as she was further exposed to the chilly air of the room. Even with her fluffy socks on, the cold of the floorboards permeated through to her toes.

Quickly, Lottie pulled out her suitcase from under the bed, unzipped it and flipped the lid. With all her clothes and the rest of her stuff now packed into the chest of drawers in the room or sat on her bedside table, the present lay obvious in the corner of the case.

Lottie grabbed it and shook it by her ear, grinning as she heard something rattle inside. Kicking the empty case back under her bed she sat back down, smiling at her present. Suddenly, she wasn't as bothered about being cold anymore. Lottie admired the purple glittery paper for a moment, before ripping it off with a flourish. It revealed a thin, posh box, adorned in black felt. Lottie's first guess was that it might contain jewellery.

Almost more interesting was the piece of paper sellotaped to the underneath of the box, folded over three times to fit neatly along the box's length. Had her mother written her a letter? How mysterious! Lottie carefully removed the piece of paper before excitedly beginning to read.

Dear Lottie,

Happy Birthday! I do hope you've managed to wait until your big day to open it, but never mind if not! I'm so sorry we couldn't be with you, love, but we hope you have a lovely day and can't wait to celebrate with you soon.

As for your present itself—this is very special, because my mother gave me this locket when I was 11 and she got it from her mother, too. It's like a family heirloom! I hope you love it as much as I have. Sending you lots of love,

Mum and Dad xxx

Lottie stared wide-eyed at the note her mother had written. She was being given a family heirloom! Her fingers traced the edges of the long black box, almost reluctant to open it because the suspense was so wonderful. If she was honest with herself, there was a part of her that was also somewhat gleeful. It was rather too childish than Lottie wanted to admit, but the truth was she was rather pleased that this heirloom had come to her and not to Nadia. Lottie grinned wickedly at the thought.

At last, then, unable to contain her excitement any longer, the girl popped open the box, the lid giving a soft click as the catch released. Lottie gasped. It was the most beautiful, mysterious object she had ever fixed her eyes upon.

Lottie had been right—it was jewellery. Lying neatly in the black box, on a bed of more soft black felt, was a locket. All of it was gold; the purest gold she had ever seen. The chain was stretched above the big heart pendant of the locket.

Carefully, holding her breath, Lottie took the locket out of its case. The girl held the top of the chain with the thumb and forefinger of her left hand, letting the locket twirl gently. The girl frowned, then smiled. It certainly was a mysterious and strange present, but it was also truly beautiful. Lottie was looking forward to asking her mother about it when she saw her again. As her heart skipped a beat, she clicked the locket open, then squashed a little disappointment to find it empty.

Just then, though, Lottie noticed the front of the locket seemed to have a few scratchings on it. At first Lottie assumed it was just where the gold had been scuffed, for she knew how soft and malleable the metal was—especially as the locket was old, passed down from other generations of family members.

As she held it closer, however, she realised that most of the markings were deeper, seeming almost deliberate. Was it some kind of engraving? Lottie held the locket closer, but with her lamp's bulb being so dim, she could hardly see it properly.

Lottie leapt to her feet, deciding at once to go to the bathroom, rather than turning on her bedroom light. Aunt Susan hadn't gone to bed yet and it would be just her luck for her aunt to come upstairs, just as she was examining the locket. The light in the bathroom was good and her aunt could hardly scold her for being in there.

She hurriedly pulled her dressing gown on and tightened the cord about her waist. Lottie carefully laid the locket back in the black box and placed it in her dressing gown pocket. The floorboards creaked under the old carpet of the landing as usual as Lottie walked to the bathroom, but she found she hardly noticed it. She was more used to it now than when she'd first arrived and besides, she was far too preoccupied in thinking about her locket, all too aware of how the box swayed against the fluffy fabric as she moved.

The walk to the bathroom seemed to take forever, but at last she reached it. Lottie closed the door and locked it, before turning on the light and taking the locket out of its box again. Once more she held the beautiful jewellery at the top of the chain, peering at it in wonder.

Yes, Lottie decided as she stood there by the bathroom sink, the etchings into the gold definitely seemed to have a pattern to them. She couldn't tell why, because there weren't any shapes she recognised, but there did seem to be a kind of order, or purpose, to the slanted lines and dots carved into the locket. A little thrill ran through Lottie at the prospect of a mystery. What were these engravings? What could they mean? She tilted the locket around gently in the light, giving a small frown.

That was when suddenly, rather than the chill that seemed to follow her everywhere in Aunt Susan's house, Lottie began to grow uncomfortably warm. The lights seemed a little brighter in here, too. Her feet shifted from one to the other on the stone bathroom floor as she blinked.

When Lottie opened her eyes again, she realised it wasn't the bathroom lights that were brighter. The locket itself seemed to be glowing, radiating a gold glow almost like sunshine. Lottie blinked again, shaking her head a little. This time when she looked, the locket was just as normal as before.

"It's just my imagination," Lottie said, only a little too loudly. A little relieved the locket seemed perfectly ordinary again, the girl turned on the tap and splashed a little cold water onto her face. There, that felt better, she thought, as her feeling of being faint faded. Lottie decided she was just being overtired; her mind was just playing tricks on her, that was it. She told herself to grow up as she absently looked from the bathroom mirror to her locket again.

"It can't be." Her voice came as a shrill whisper as she saw her locket start to glow again. She wondered if she could call to Aunt Susan, but what could she do? Lottie's eyes widened further as the bathroom sink suddenly got bigger, growing to five times its size.

"Impossible," Lottie muttered, stepping back, but the sink didn't listen as the taps stretched far and wide, as if it was about to swallow her whole.

"I must be dreaming!" She cried, feeling some kind of force behind her, pushing her towards the sink. Before Lottie could even think about what to do next, suddenly there was a blinding flash of gold light and she vanished from the face of the earth.

***

Wet, everywhere. It was cool, rather than cold. A strange light filtering through her closed eyelids. These were Lottie's first impressions of wherever she was. Instantly, Lottie realised she was fully submerged in water and panic threatened to overcome her. Where was she? What had happened? She had been standing in Aunt Susan's bathroom, hadn't she? Had the old house flooded somehow? It hadn't even been raining!

A moment later Lottie became aware she had been fighting against the water. Her lungs were growing a little tighter now from holding her breath. Fortunately, she was a very strong swimmer. Lottie forced herself to calm down, making little controlled movements with her arms and legs, gliding up through the water. Absently, she noticed it felt different. Thicker, somehow, but far thinner than mud. As her lungs tightened still, Lottie swam faster, all other questions fleeing to the back of her mind. The only thing to concentrate on was getting air again.

Just as Lottie began to grow really scared that she might drown, she suddenly broke free of the water. Her arms writhed in relief as she inhaled clear air, before suddenly submerging again. The girl fought as hard as she could against her panic, slowly propelling herself to the surface again. Lottie forced herself to be as still as she could, gently swishing her arms to maintain buoyancy, growing calm as she breathed slowly. Air had never tasted so delicious, as she sucked it back into her lungs. Out of caution more than anything else, Lottie kept her eyes shut.

"Oh, my goodness!" She heard someone call. Dimly, in a part of her brain that was still functioning, Lottie registered that the voice was not Aunt Susan's. In fact, she had never heard that voice before. It sounded different to anyone she had ever heard. "Are you all right?" Lottie coughed.

"I... I think so," she managed to rasp, so quietly she wasn't sure her voice had made it to whoever was talking to her. While keeping one arm moving in the water, Lottie raised the other hand to wipe her face weakly. This done, Lottie at last risked opening her eyes. Then she screamed.

The shock of what she saw was almost enough to send her

below the surface again, but her swimmer's instinct kept her afloat. Shaking, Lottie tried to take it all in. The water around her was pure gold, like nothing she had ever seen before. High above her was the wide expanse of a cavern. The black stone of the cave roof gleamed as it reflected lit torches, suspended all around.

"Please, don't distress yourself!" Lottie gasped, almost screaming again, as the speaker now came into view. At once she knew it wasn't human. The creature was vivid blue, but its skin was also sparkled with gold, a similar hue to that of the water. It wore (were those clothes?) a dark grey sort of dress. The girl assumed again she must be dreaming, but her fear of drowning had been so terrifying and real, surely it would have woken her up.

Lottie went to speak again, but a small current coming towards her made some of the water enter her mouth. She spat it out before she choked, but not before she tasted the strong flavour. The water was like strong mineral water, except with the faint sweetness of honey. Lottie wasn't sure she liked it at all.

"It's a girl! A human being!" As the tall one spoke, a new person came into view, much smaller. Lottie guessed the second creature was of similar height to herself, also with bright blue skin and hair that was short and bright orange. Lottie blinked, unable to make sense of how shocked the taller one had sounded. Since when had a human girl been surprising?

"Stop it, mum, you're scaring her," the younger one said, patting the taller one's arm. The smaller one stepped forward. "Can you swim over? Don't worry, we're not going to hurt you." Something like logic fired in Lottie's brain. Wherever she was, whether this was a dream or not, she couldn't stay in this gold pond forever.

"All right," Lottie decided. It only took her a few seconds to swim quickly over to the rocky floor, where the two blue creatures stood watching. Concern and surprise were painted on both of their faces, as the younger one approached her.

"Here," the smaller creature said, holding out a hand. Apart from the gold and blue speckled skin, Lottie thought the hand looked ordinary enough. Hesitantly, Lottie accepted it and the younger creature pulled Lottie free from the water and onto the rocky floor.

"Don't speak for a moment—catch your breath," the older one suggested, gently. Lottie panted, bewildered, on her hands and knees on the cave floor. She swallowed, running a hand over her mouth. Then Lottie watched in awe, as the water all over her seemed to change. The thick golden droplets suddenly jumped towards one another, as if magnetically attracted to one another. Except it wasn't metal, Lottie reminded herself. It was water.

"You'll be all right in a minute." It was the older one who spoke, her tone quiet and calming. Lottie took comfort in how kind and concerned both voices had sounded so far. "I'm Guira. This is my daughter, Zara," she introduced. "What's your name?"

"Lottie." She sat back, looking at the cavern full of the gold water. Then, to her right, she could make out a soft orange sky out of the mouth of the cave. At a guess, it seemed to be sunset here. Wherever here was. Lottie swallowed again, the faint taste of minerals and honey still in her mouth. She glanced back to the blue lady and her daughter.

"Where am I?" Lottie asked, her voice a little stronger.

33

"How did I get here? What's happened to me?" Absently, she noticed the gold droplets continued to jump towards each other.

"You are in the realm known as Orovand," Guira answered. "Otherwise known as the Gold Dimension. You must have been brought here by your locket."

"The locket!" Lottie cried as she remembered. She reached into her dressing gown pocket. The black box was there, but she knew it would be empty. The last thing she remembered was holding it in front of the bathroom sink, then nothing.

"Don't worry, it's safe," said Zara. Lottie looked at her. "We needed your locket for the ceremony. You'll get it back later," she added with a quick smile. Lottie frowned.

"What?" Lottie coughed, leaning against a boulder as she got to her feet. "What ceremony? The locket is mine," she pointed out. She looked down at her dressing gown as the gold droplets continued to swiftly blob together before jumping to the floor. In effect, she was already almost dry.

"Of course it is," Guira agreed. "I'm sorry, this must be so distressing for you." The blue lady clucked her tongue in sympathy. "Please know you are safe and welcome in our world. All of the lockets are over there, look," Guira said, pointing.

Lottie dubiously followed the blue lady's finger. She saw fifty or so lockets looking almost identical to hers, hanging from hooks that seemed to be carved into the wall of the cave. Stood in front of them was a large man, with the same blue skin that they had. Well, almost the same—his skin seemed to be richer and darker, like navy. His hair was long and the colour of raspberry jam, flecked with gold like Guira and

Zara's hair and skin were.

She noticed he was staring back at her just as intently, but Lottie realised she'd be gawping at him, as if he'd suddenly appeared out of nowhere in a gold pond. As she caught his eye, he did not smile, but gracefully nodded his head towards her.

"That's Preto," Zara said. Lottie jumped at the blue girl suddenly beside her. "Sorry," she apologised with another small smile. "Preto's job is the Guardian of the Lockets. He makes sure nobody does anything to them until after the ceremony tonight, when they go back to your world."

"The lockets form a link between your world and ours," Guira explained now. "Your locket helps power our world."

"You take power from our world?" Lottie stepped back, looking between the blue lady and her daughter with a frown. "Do you steal it?"

"No, of course not," Guira was quick to reply, but the friendly smile remained on her face. "The powering of Orovand happens naturally through the power of the lockets." Lottie's face creased further, more confused than ever.

"Let me ask you a question," Guira said. "What does gold mean to you?" Lottie thought for a moment, then gave a little shrug.

"It's nice," she answered vaguely. "People in my world find it in the ground. It's quite expensive, used in jewellery, like rings and stuff. It can also be used as money," she added.

"You would not, though, I believe, see it as integral for your existence," Guira pointed out. "It is for us, you see. I do not think our world sees gold the way you do," the blue lady suggested.

"Mum, it's easier to show her," Zara stated, tugging at her mother's wrist. "Come on, let's show you around." Guira nodded.

"Yes, let us show you our world, Lottie," Guira invited. "Then you might perhaps understand. Preto," she added, "we will see you here later, for the ceremony." Preto still didn't speak, but only nodded his head again.

"Unless you want to spend your whole time in this cave?" Zara said, gently teasing. For the first time since her arrival in this strange new world, Lottie found a smile twitching at her lips.

"Not really," Lottie replied. Zara grinned as the three of them made their way out of the cave. "Wait!" the girl suddenly called, stepping back. The other two looked back to see was distractedly pulling her dressing gown round her. "I'm in my pyjamas," Lottie explained, clearly flustered as she tied the fluffy cord around her dressing gown. She was suddenly very grateful she'd put her dressing gown on when she'd gone to the bathroom, because that at least gave her a little more dignity—although she wasn't sure she could say the same about her purple fluffy socks.

"Don't worry about that," Guira smiled reassuringly, whilst Zara giggled. "We're all so excited to see you, nobody will care what you're wearing. You look like you're the same size as Zara—you can borrow some of her clothes to wear later, if you like."

"Sure," Zara beamed. "Besides, even your pyjamas look totally different to what we would wear. You could always say they're your official robes or something." Lottie smirked.

"All right, then," Lottie agreed, only a little hesitantly. After all, it would be slightly ridiculous to have come to a new world only to stay in the cave because she didn't have anything to wear.

With that, the three of them crossed the cavern floor, Lottie watching she didn't trip up on the loose stones in her fluffy socks. As they neared the mouth of the cave, the girl caught her first glimpse of the world outside. Below the orange of the sunset sky, Lottie saw there was a dense forest. As she looked closer, she frowned.

"Turquoise," Lottie murmured to herself. She then glanced to Guira and Zara, realising she had spoken aloud. "The trees are all bright turquoise," she said, louder, as if that explained it. Never had she seen woodland looking so vivid and resplendent. "The grass, too!" Lottie almost shouted, pointing at the turquoise tufts outside the cavern, as they came into view.

"Of course they are," Zara said, giving Lottie a funny look. "What colour were you expecting them to be? Purple, like your socks?" she teased.

"Don't be unkind, Zara," Guira admonished, turning to reprimand her daughter. "I'm sure if we came to Lottie's world, things would look a lot different to us. What colour are they in your world?" the blue lady asked, looking interested.

"Green," Lottie replied, looking at the trees in wonder. "Like a dark green, although some of them are lighter…" the girl stopped mid-sentence, her voice trailing away into a silent awe. The three of them had at last left the cavern and Lottie's mouth hung open in wonder, utterly transfixed.

"It's so beautiful," Lottie whispered hoarsely. Right then, she knew 'beautiful' was totally inadequate. 'Magnificent' would come closer, but still it didn't do what she was seeing justice. Lottie wished for better adjectives to get to the essence of this world she was witnessing. The turquoise forest looked like it would go on forever, underneath the sunset that was far more intense than she could have imagined. There was a simple path that led from the cavern, cutting right through the forest, that led all the way to a vast, golden roof in the distance that Lottie couldn't quite make out.

Looking at the view in front of her, Lottie bit her lip, but it wasn't out of anxiety. Rather, as she stared out into this new world, she felt all her usual worries melt away. Guira had called this a different realm. Lottie had wanted to go on an adventure—this was it. Suddenly, none of the questions about how and why she came to be here mattered. Instead, she simply marvelled in gratitude at whatever magic had brought her here.

"I'm glad you like it," Guira smiled. "Come on, let's get back to town," she added, gesturing to the path in front of them that wound through the woods. "You must be tired after your adventure getting here. Besides, if those are your pyjamas, then it looks like you were ready for bed," she deduced, glancing to Lottie's attire.

"Oh, Mum, you can't make her go to bed now, she's just arrived!" Zara protested immediately. "Besides, she has to come to the ceremony and the feast. The king will probably have her as an honoured guest."

"There's a king?" Lottie gasped as they walked, looking between them. "Is Orovand a magical kingdom?" She was filled with excitement and wonder, in equal measure.

"I suppose the lockets are magical," Guira agreed with a grin, "but the way of things here seems normal to us! As to your question, yes, King Karalius rules over all Orovand. We are just outside the capital city, Oruvesi. We'll be able to see it in a minute, when we've cleared the forest."

"Mum works for the king," Zara supplied as they walked

along, "as one of his court advisors. We live in some rooms at one end of the palace."

"You live there?" Lottie echoed, then realised she was asking about pretty much everything they said. "That's cool," she simply said with a smile, not wanting to annoy them with too many questions, five minutes after she'd arrived here.

"I think so," Zara grinned broadly, making her mother smile. "Here's the clearing!" she added, pointing in front of them. "You can see almost the whole kingdom from here. Come on!" With that she broke into a run, racing off towards the vantage point.

"Always full of energy," Guira mused, shaking her head as Zara run on a few feet before stopping. Lottie broke into a jog to catch up before coming to a complete halt herself, stilled by the awe and wonder washing over her like waves.

Chapter Three

"Welcome to Orovand," Zara said, grinning as she stretched her arms out towards the sprawling turquoise fields below. Lottie gazed at the wondrous landscape before her, riveted by the raw beauty of this magical new world. At last, her mouth curved into a smile, her throat too tight for words. Lottie was having her new adventure after all.

The new human girl to this realm took in all she could, keeping her eyes peeled open until they went watery. As soon as she had to blink, they were open wide once more, desperate not to miss this wonderful world a moment longer than she had to.

Lottie could see now why they called Orovand the 'Gold Dimension'. Every single building of the city was flecked with gold, as were the roads and pavements. The whole capital was sparkling like the way the surface of the ocean glistens and dapples with burning orange at sunset.

Higher than all the city's buildings, was the towering palace that she'd only just been able to glimpse outside the cave. From this vantage point, Lottie could also see the boundary of one edge of the city. Beyond it were sloping hills, all with the same vivid turquoise as the grass outside the cavern.

Further afield, she could just make out the glimmering of a body of water, shimmering in the distance. Lottie thought to comment, but instead she only swallowed. Suddenly, she realised she was close to tears at the sight of it all.

"Are you all right, Lottie?" Guira asked quietly. Lottie only nodded in response. She still didn't trust her voice enough to speak. "In the cave, I said that your world maybe doesn't view gold in the way we do. For us, gold is integral for our very existence," she began to explain. "It's in our water, in all our buildings and the earth beneath us… it's in our very bloodstream." Lottie tore her eyes away from the majesty of all that was before her to look at Guira, wanting to pay close attention to what Orovand was like and how it worked.

"The gold from your world powers ours," Guira continued. "The two are inextricably linked. When all the lockets are together, they begin to glow and form the link between Earth and the Golden Dimension. They do this one night every year, during the Ceremony of the Lockets."

"Yours is one of fifty lockets in your world," Zara chimed in. "Every year at the ceremony, they leave your world to appear in Orovand. I don't really understand the physics of it," Zara added, shrugging. "Centuries ago, scientists working in Oruvesi figured out a way to draw power from the gold in Earth that then channels into the gold here. It keeps Orovand alive. You'll see for yourself," Zara said, glancing hopefully to her mother.

"I'm sure the king would want your presence at the ceremony," Guira agreed, shooting a wry smile at her daughter. "You must tell us, though, Lottie, if you get too tired."

"Sure," Lottie agreed, privately wondering how she would be able to sleep a single wink while she was in the Gold Dimension.

41

"That's the Purua Lake you can see in the distance," Guira said, pointing to the shimmering water Lottie had spied a few moments' earlier. "Across the lake, a day's sail away, are our other two cities. There's Edowoda to the west and Tilajin to the south." Guira dropped her hand a moment to glance at Lottie. "The other cities have existed in peaceful harmony for centuries."

"To the east," said Zara, pointing, "you should just be able to make out the start of the Mavi Mountains, next to the lake." Lottie followed her new friends' gaze. Across the lake, Lottie could just spy out the formidable forms of the mountains towering. They were a deep blue, even darker looking than the sky above her.

"The caps of the mountains are gold!" Lottie gasped. She could make out just the start of the tops of the peaks, before they disappeared into the misty clouds above them. "Because all the water is gold," she then reasoned with a frown, working it out for herself.

"Of course!" Lottie then grinned excitedly to Zara. "That must mean it rains and snows gold here, too!" She was filled with wonder anew at the thought of golden droplets descending to the ground. Zara giggled and Lottie realised once more she was stating the obvious.

"That's right, Lottie," Guira encouraged with a smile. "You're beginning to see how it works. Shall we head back to the city?" she suggested. The three of them made their way along the path, with towering turquoise trees lining each side.

Lottie had been a bit anxious about walking through woodland with fluffy socks, where she might hurt her feet on loose pebbles, but her new blue friend had been right. Looking down, Lottie saw the path had a layer of very fine, soft gravel.

It was like walking on sand. As she peered closer, she saw even the gravel was flecked with gold. "What's the water like in your world, then?" Zara now asked, interested. Lottie glanced back up at her.

"It's sort of see through," Lottie answered, trying to think of the best way to describe it. "It tastes like a very weak version of yours, without being sweet."

"Water that doesn't taste sweet?" Zara echoed, then shrugged. "Sounds boring. Sorry, Mum," she said quickly to her mother, who quickly raised an eyebrow, looking ready to rebuke her again.

"It sort of, is, actually," Lottie agreed. "I like the taste of it, but lots of my friends add squash to their water. That's like sugar, I guess, that comes in different flavours. Usually fruit," she added to Zara's confused expression.

"Do you squash the water, before you drink it?" Zara asked. At this, Lottie laughed and shook her head, grinning.

"No, I don't know why it's called squash, really. Maybe because they squash the fruit," she wondered aloud, still giggling.

As they walked, Lottie suddenly realised what her hair must look like and rose her hands to her head. Sure enough, part of her ponytail had come loose and lots of her wavy hair had gone scraggly. Lottie pulled the band free with a flourish, slipping it through her wrist. She was amazed that her hair was hardly damp; Lottie decided they may have no need for towels in Orovand. Trying to look more respectable (which was no easy task considering her purple fluffy socks), Lottie ran her hands through her hair a few times and gathered it back in her hands again.

"You're a really good swimmer, by the way," Zara

complimented as they neared the city. Lottie smiled as she glanced at her new friend, hands still full with hair.

"Thanks. It's one of my favourite things to do." As she spoke, Lottie expertly flipped her band around her hair, tightening it into a ponytail. Then, as they rounded a bend in the path, Lottie's arms dropped to her sides, her mouth open wide once more; her worry about her appearance totally forgotten.

"Here we are, then," Guira announced brightly, as they came to the vast city wall of Oruvesi. Lottie's mouth twitched a little. The cheery tone reminded her of her mother. The girl stared at the huge ornate pillars that stood either side of the gate, cut into the city wall. To her left and right, the wall (every brick flecked with gold, of course) seemed to stretch on forever. She assumed it probably went all the way around the city.

Lottie took a few steps forward, gasping as she marvelled at what lay on the other side of the gate. The first thing she saw was gleaming golden cobbles, which then smoothed out into a proper road, with neat pavements either side. Raising her eyes higher, Lottie saw the road led to three junctions.

"Everything's just…" Lottie swallowed, hardly able to process or even express her emotions. "Wonderful," she ended with a grin.

"Welcome to Oruvesi," Zara beamed, obviously delighted her new friend found her home so marvellous. "Come on, it's not far to the centre, then you can see the palace." Lottie followed them, glancing sideways at Guira and Zara as a thought occurred to her.

"You don't seem as shocked to see me as I am to see you," Lottie observed now. "I'm not the first human to have come here, am I?"

"You're not the first human to come here, no," Guira agreed, her blue arms swaying gently as she walked. "Although it is very rare. The last time a human came here was a hundred years ago."

"Wow, a hundred years?" Lottie almost choked on the words as she repeated them. "That explains why you were a bit surprised to see me," she added and Zara grinned. "How did I get here, then?" Lottie asked next, frowning as she thought. "You said it was because of the locket."

"Yes," Guira answered, nodding. "Occasionally, if there is a strong link between the human and the locket, there is enough power generated to bring the human through to this world," Guira explained. "My mother remembered well the last time a human came. She was a child, like you." Lottie rose her eyebrows a little at this, thinking maybe people lived longer here in Orovand than in the real world. "It's so long ago now that people are beginning to think it was just a myth—"

"Lottie's just proved it, though, hasn't she, Mum?" Zara chimed in, excitedly. "She's proved it's possible for humans to come to our world."

"She certainly has," Guira smiled. She then glanced at Lottie with interest, folding her arms. "There are historical records of only five human visitors. It's curious that all of them have been children. When the last child came," Guira added, "our scientists discovered she had a small amount of gold in her bloodstream. Completely harmless to her, of course," the wise blue lady said. "Probably not even detectable to Earth's scientists. It's probable you have the same gold in your bloodstream, too."

"What?" Lottie came to a sudden stop, casting her

shocked gaze to Guira. They had now almost come to the end of the cobbles. They had been bumpy but hadn't hurt her feet, still clad only in her fluffy purple socks. "Are you saying that I have this gold blood too?"

"Well, unless there's another way for humans to come to our world we haven't discovered yet." Guira had also come to a stop and smiled reassuringly. "Don't worry—as I said, it's completely safe. The girl who came here before, she ate and drank everything we did." Lottie nodded as they began walking again. She thought she could probably trust her new friends, but Guira herself had just said the last human that came here was a hundred years ago. If the people of Orovand were beginning to doubt everything that happened because it was so long ago, then how could Lottie trust that anything was safe for her?

"Mum!" Zara muttered suddenly, as she nearly walked into her mother. Lottie stopped beside her friends, noticing Guira had a very faraway expression on her face.

"Ah, I wonder," Guira said suddenly. She turned to peer at Lottie, still deep in thought. "It's possible the gold in your bloodstream was genetically passed on." Then her face changed as her eyes widened, her blue and gold-speckled face breaking into a broad smile. "Yes, of course! Why didn't I notice it before!"

"What are you talking about?" Lottie protested, bemused. She was beginning to feel a bit tired of having to ask so many questions about everything to do with Orovand. "Genetically passed on…" Lottie frowned, her voice trailing away. "Are you telling me my parents have gold in their bloodstreams, too?"

"More than that… don't you notice it, Zara, from the

paintings?" Guira asked her daughter eagerly. "That same small pointed nose, the same curve of the chin." Her daughter's eyes widened, as she nodded quickly. "Tell me, Lottie," she said breathlessly. "What is your mother called?"

"My mother?" Lottie questioned. "She's just…" her voice faded again as she twigged where Guira was heading with the sudden change in conversation. "You think my mum is the girl that came here a hundred years ago? She's only forty-one," Lottie protested. Guira gave a small nod but said nothing, waiting for her to answer the question.

"Her name's Julie," Lottie at last admitted, with a bemused smile. "Julie Armitage. Wait," she added. "You mean her name before she married my dad," she said, trying to remember her mother's maiden name. "Her name was Julie Sawyer."

"Julie Sawyer," gasped Zara, as the two stepped back, looking at her in renewed shock and delight. "It's true, Mum!" Zara shrieked, moving to clap her hands. Lottie stared between them, her confusion only growing at their reaction. Her mum couldn't have come to Orovand, could she?

"The name of the child who came here a hundred years ago," Guira said, her voice still a little quick, "was Julie Sawyer. She was eleven at the time. She was your mother," she declared.

"What!" Lottie's eyes struck open, stunned. "Like I said, my mum wasn't even alive then! It must be a coincidence," she said.

Even as she spoke, she knew this was incredibly unlikely, given her locket was an heirloom. After all, how many other girls called Julie Sawyer would have a magical locket? Lottie had been learning about her family tree only a few weeks ago,

47

so she knew she didn't have any ancestors called Julie Sawyer, as far as she knew.

"We always assumed your world travelled at the same pace as ours," Guira spoke now, her voice a little calmer, "but maybe it doesn't. Maybe time moves much more slowly here in Orovand than on Earth." Lottie barely heard the words Guira was saying. Her mouth was still hung open, at the thought her mother had come to this magical world.

"I'm eleven today," she stammered, for she could think of nothing else to say. "You're saying my mother was here, in this world, when she was my age?"

"Most definitely," Zara grinned, nodding. "You look a lot like your mum, too, which makes sense," she joked. Lottie frowned, remembering how a few seconds ago Guira had talked about Lottie's nose and chin. That was what people often commented on, when they talked about her family resemblance.

"I'm sorry, Lottie, I know this is a lot to take in," Guira muttered, a thread of an apology now in her voice. Lottie gave a small smile, thankful for her guide's tact. "You said your mother is forty-one now," Guira added, a little louder. "That means thirty years have passed in your world, when a whole century has passed in ours."

"Happy birthday, by the way!" Zara added brightly here, as mother and daughter continued to lead Lottie towards the palace. Cautiously, Lottie followed them along the gold paved road.

"Thanks." Lottie tried to smile back at her new friend, but she was struggling to take it all in. Was she really about to meet the king who ruled over everything here? Lottie bit her lip, feeling her anxiety settle in again. Guira and Zara seemed friendly enough, but suddenly Lottie wasn't sure she even wanted to be here, despite being on a new adventure and how beautiful everything was.

It was the revelation her mother had come here before her thirty years ago (or a hundred, from the Gold Dimension's point of view) that had really thrown her. Could her mother, Julie Sawyer as she was known then, have come to this magical realm and never breathed a word to her? Lottie wondered whether her mum had been told to keep it a secret. Or perhaps this was an experience you had to live through yourself, rather than be told about it. After all, Lottie decided, if her mum had warned her that her mysterious heirloom would take her to a magical dimension, Lottie would never have believed it.

Still feeling a little vulnerable, Lottie looked away, not wanting to show Guira and Zara how overwhelmed she felt. Instead, she distracted herself by admiring the beautiful buildings. Apart from the obvious difference that everything was gold, Lottie decided things didn't look too dissimilar from a city on Earth. There were towering skyscrapers, as well as smaller buildings—Lottie thought they were probably like the offices in cities and towns back home. Then there were even smaller buildings that looked like houses, in pretty shades of pale pink, white, or light blue. Each one of them, like every other atom that existed here, was flecked with the same gold that powered the realm.

As they passed a square, Lottie noticed there was a kind of market being packed up. It looked so normal that it was a comforting sight. She liked to think that even if it was a strange new realm, there were ordinary people living here, eating and drinking and buying and selling, going about their lives. As the delicious smells of whatever food was being sold grew stronger, Lottie's stomach rumbled. Zara giggled.

"Are you hungry, Lottie?" Guira smiled at her warmly. "The feast won't be until later, so you're welcome to a snack to keep you going if you like." Lottie hesitated, but then remembered the human girl who had come here was no longer a myth, but her very own mother. If her mum had been able to able and drink here without being poisoned by anything, then surely so could she.

"All right, then, thanks," Lottie agreed, with a shy smile of her own. As they crossed the square together to a small stall still doing business, she felt something resolve inside her. Here she was in a brand-new world, to be under a different sun and have the magical adventure she'd always dreamed of when she was little. Lottie decided, as much as she could, to enjoy this wonderful experience, rather than giving in to all her worries and anxieties. Lottie knew it would be hard, but... yes, she decided to try. With that, Lottie took her final, determined step and came to a stop in front of the market stall.

"Dendari, good to see you," Guira greeted as they came to a stop outside the stall. The trader had his head down, writing something on a piece of paper, but he nodded. "You might notice we have a rather special visitor with us," Guira added. At this Dendari looked up, his eyes widening at once as he spotted Lottie, who smiled shyly at him in response.

"Orovand's gold," he said. "How exciting! Sorry," he added and grinned. "I was just finishing up my business records for the day... never mind that, what's your name?" he asked, putting his pen behind his ear. "Have you just come through the portal? Obviously, you have," he beamed.

"Uh, yeah," Lottie replied and smiled again. "My name's

Lottie." The man smiled back as he reached forward to shake her hand. Lottie noticed that though his skin was the same bright blue as Guira and Zara's, his hair was darker than anyone else she'd met. It looked almost black, but it was still peppered with gold. His broad grin was so contagious Lottie couldn't help but keep smiling back. "We haven't had a human here in—"

"A hundred years!" Zara finished for him excitedly, looking almost gleeful. "What's more, Lottie is the daughter of Julie Sawyer!"

"Is that so?" Dendari asked, looking positively amazed. "Well, it's quite an honour to meet you, Miss Lottie. Would you care for some refreshment? Here, this is something you might like. It's a sort of speciality of mine, called a cronzaki." Dendari gave her a wink as he held out what looked to be a pretzel, but far bigger. As Lottie took it from him, she noticed it was a different shape, too—this almost looked like a Celtic cross. It was quite warm, so Lottie held on to the paper wrapping of the snack carefully.

"Don't worry about price," he added, as Guira plucked out a purse from her long, swaying jacket. "Consider it a gift! It's not every day you meet a human from Earth. Consider it my welcome to Orovand," he added, sweeping an arm around him to gesture the magical realm.

"Thank you very much." Lottie smiled once more as Guira put her purse away. If everybody was going to be this friendly, she thought, then maybe she wouldn't have any problems at all meeting new people in Orovand.

"It smells delicious," Lottie said, because it really, really did. The top of the cronzaki was sprinkled with salt, which smelt so fresh she could have been by the seaside. The girl was still a little a bit hesitant about trying totally alien food, but her senses were so won over that she couldn't help but take the first, tiny bite.

Lottie had been right to guess it was like a pretzel—the hard, salty, outer surface of the snack was definitely familiar, even if tasted a little different. Encouraged, she took a much larger bite.

"Wow," Lottie murmured in delight, hardly noticing she had done her mother's pet peeve of speaking with her mouth full. The crunchiness of the outside gave way to the fluffiest, creamiest sponge cake she had ever tasted. The sponge tasted like it was lightly flavoured with spices, perhaps something like cinnamon. This was mixed with something else in the middle of the cronzaki—something like custard, flavoursome but not overly rich. Altogether, it was one of the most wonderful things she had ever eaten.

"This is amazing," Lottie grinned, swallowing the first heavenly mouthful. Now she had started the snack, she had to resist every temptation to eat it as quickly as possible.

"You're most welcome." Dendari smiled. "I won't keep you any longer, I'm afraid," he continued, moving to start packing away the boxes of his stall. "I still have some preparing to do for the catering tonight," he added to Guira.

"See you later, at the feast!" Zara called loudly, as Guira said goodbye to the baker. The three of them then left the square, still heading towards the palace. Lottie savoured another delicious mouthful, then sniffed again the wonderful snack. "I love cronzakis," Zara said wistfully, glancing in Lottie's direction.

"I know, dear," Guira replied with a wink, a joke rebuke laced through her tone. "I gave you a massive lunch though, remember? So you could last until the feast." Zara nodded, but she still looked longingly at the cronzaki in Lottie's hand.

"Besides," Guira chuckled, winding a hand round her daughter's shoulder, "Dendari will be bringing lots more today, miniature ones for after the feast. He makes quite a trade," she added to Lottie, who only nodded, enjoying another heavenly mouthful.

"Look, here it is now," Zara pointed, stepping forwards from her mum's embrace as they reached the end of a pretty street with tall houses either side, revealing the biggest, grandest, most beautiful building Lottie had ever seen. At last, she had come to the royal palace in Oruvesi.

Chapter Four

For what felt like the umpteenth time, Lottie came to a standstill, in awe at the sight of the palace. The part of the palace's roof she'd been able to spy from outside the cave should have told her something about its gigantic size, but it was still much bigger than she'd been expecting. Unlike the other buildings in the city that were flecked or speckled with gold, the palace was thick, gold stone. The sun, finally about to dip below the horizon, shone all its deep, remaining light onto the palace. Indeed, the whole grand building gleamed so intensely it looked like it was ablaze.

Lottie could see there were ten large windows, five on each side of the ornate doors that looked like the one on the city wall. They were half the height of the palace wall, looking as though they were the purest crystal, shimmering brightly like dust caught in a sunbeam.

Then her eyes caught movement to her left and though her cronzaki was one of the most heavenly things she'd ever eaten, Lottie nearly dropped it. A grand white carriage was pulling into view. Although it was the most beautiful carriage Lottie had ever seen, she hardly paid it any attention. Instead, Lottie was more transfixed by the creatures that were pulling the carriage long. The slender, majestic animals were no mere horses—their unique horns were unmistakable.

"Unicorns!" Lottie shrieked in delight. For once, she

forgot about any sense of shyness or decorum. Any anxiety or questions about this new world fled from her mind as she raced towards the side of the carriage, which stopped as soon as she neared it.

"Hey, do you mind?" a cross voice snapped, as a man got out of the front of the carriage, a frown set into the deep blue of his face, looking down as he lowered the reins. "I nearly ran you over—" the man stopped in his tracks as he turned around to face her properly.

"Are you all right, Lottie?" Guira asked a little breathlessly, as she and Zara stopped beside her. "This is Karoc," Guira introduced. "He's the head carriage driver in Oruvesi."

"You're human," Karoc stated obviously. Lottie didn't know what to say, so she only nodded. "You came here because of the lockets?" he guessed. Lottie nodded again. Then, to her surprise, his eyes hardened. "Well, let me give you a piece of advice—watch out for the roads and make sure the carriages come to a stop first. You could have been hurt." He breathed noisily through his nostrils as he spoke, his anger clear. Lottie almost took a step back at the direct, unkind tone to his voice.

"Hardly, you'd already stopped," Zara pointed out huffily. Karoc turned his beady eyes to her, roving a hand through his soft blonde hair.

"Don't be rude, Zara," Guira said, but Lottie thought the rebuke sounded hollow, done more out of necessity rather than being cross with her daughter. "I think she was just excited to see the unicorns," she added. Guira had kept her smile, but her voice sounded firmer.

"Yes," Lottie murmured, glancing to the beautiful

creatures rather than to the grumpy carriage driver. As magnificent as the creatures were, though, the way Karoc had spoken to her still stung. It was as if the moment was spoilt, somehow. Lottie didn't know how to get the initial feeling of magic and wonder back again.

"That's all as well," Karoc replied grumpily. "I'm just telling her to be careful, that's all." Karoc folded his arms. "Your name's Lottie, then?" The carriage driver's voice had changed a little, but it was more 'less grumpy' than it was kind, like an adult trying too hard to be nice. "Welcome to Orovand," he added, with the first real smile crossing his face. "You like unicorns?"

"Thank you, yes," Lottie replied in a small voice, appreciating Karoc was trying to talk to her. "We don't have unicorns in our world," she said. "I read somewhere on Earth some people think they might have existed, thousands of years ago, but most people think the idea of unicorns is a myth. They're often associated with magic," Lottie explained.

"How fascinating," Guira remarked. "Sometimes we wonder whether Earth and the Gold Dimension are more linked than we think," she commented. "Maybe if unicorns didn't really exist on Earth, humans got the idea of them from here."

"Maybe," Lottie murmured in agreement. Now that the awkwardness with the carriage driver seemed over, she was at last able to fully marvel at these wonderful creatures, ancient myths and folklore back on Earth but real, living animals here in Orovand.

The two unicorns, standing gracefully beside by the white carriage, were far more than horses with horns. They had the sleekest coats Lottie had ever seen. The first one was white, with a gold pattern rippled across its back. Its mane and tale were so wispy and delicate it looked like it was made from feathers. As Lottie stared, the white one bent its graceful neck, pawing the ground with a hoof just like an ordinary horse would.

The second unicorn's coat was entirely black, but with white hooves and a bright white streak across of its forehead, at the base of the horn. Its mane and tail were also a brilliant white. The white streaks across the unicorn's back were dusted with gold. It hit her again that everything in this world had gold in it, including the people. Even her, if it was true that she had gold in her blood, genetically passed down from her mother. As Lottie tore her gaze away to look back to Guira and Zara, she knew that the locket ceremony must be integral to Orovand's continued existence.

"Your world really needs this ceremony, doesn't it? Lottie asked. "What would happen if the lockets stopped working, if you couldn't get the power from Earth?" She dared to ask the sobering question, although she could probably guess the answer. Karoc the carriage driver had already turned away, attending to some task or other in his carriage.

"Yes, we do need it," Guira answered simply, her tone also growing serious. "Without the ceremony, the gold here would start to fade. Soon it would be gone altogether… then so would we."

"In that case," Lottie decided, "you're welcome to borrow my locket, for as long as it takes to power your world." It occurred to her then that it was a bit silly in a sense to give them permission, seeing as her locket was already with all the others in the cave, but she wanted them to know she was all right about it.

"Thank you so much, Lottie," Guira said warmly, appreciating the thought behind her words. "It's so very important to us that you're happy while you're here." Zara was beaming, nodding quickly beside her mother. "If you're ready, we could take you into the palace now? His Majesty King Karalius will want to meet you," Guira added.

"Um, all right, then," Lottie replied, a little reluctantly. She could feel her anxiety settling in again. It was all very well trying not to be worried about her new adventure, but she was about to meet the king over all the realm! She told herself anybody would be nervous.

"Don't worry," Zara murmured kindly as the three of them made their way up the palace steps, just reaching the huge ornate doors as the last glimmer of the sun finally dipped below the horizon. "King Karalius is a good, fair king. In fact, I'm friends with his son, Prince Andri. You'll meet him soon, too," she chattered, as she walked easily through the palace.

Lottie only nodded, imagining what it must be like to live in a palace, to stroll through these grand rooms as if they belonged to you. The main hall of the palace was huge and there was a walkway of plush burgundy carpet, the softest Lottie had ever felt. Suddenly, she was aware again of her fluffy purple socks and dressing gown, glancing down in dismay to tighten the cord about her waist.

"Mum, maybe Lottie would like to change first," Zara suggested tactfully, seeing Lottie's flustered attempts to make herself look more respectable. "After all, I doubt I'd want to meet the king in my nightdress," she said with a wink, causing the corners of Lottie's mouth to twitch into a smile, despite her cheeks being a little red still.

"Ah of course, I'm sure His Majesty won't mind. Why

don't you go show Lottie to your room and lend her one of your dresses, while I tell the king you're here?" Guira suggested.

"Sure. Come on, it's this way," Zara gestured with one arm as they proceeded across the furnished floor. At the other end of the hall was a large staircase, also lined with burgundy carpet.

"Thanks," Lottie told her new friend quietly, slipping her hands into her dressing gown pockets. As she did, she suddenly remembered her snack that she'd put there from Dendari. She'd only eaten about half of it before spotting the unicorns. Her senses came to life as she sniffed it again and took a big, comforting bite.

"I totally understand," Zara was saying, as she led them along an upstairs corridor, again fitted with red carpet. On the walls hung landscapes of Orovand and lines of portraits of people who looked very important.

"Cronzakis are one of my favourites," Zara mused dreamily. "I'd eat them every day if I could." Lottie grinned.

"I can see why." Her fluffy socks padded gently onto the soft carpet as they walked. "Who are all these people?" Lottie asked, after swallowing a mouthful of cronzaki.

"Oh, just people who have served the King in some noble, grand way." Zara sounded bored. "I'm sure lots of them have done really good things for Oruvesi, actually," she said reproachfully. "These paintings are all really old, though. I'm not sure if even my mum knows who they are. "I'm twelve in a few months, by the way," she added suddenly, "so we're pretty much the same age. Here, this is my room," Zara announced, opening the door to let them in.

"Wow," Lottie admired, as she crossed the doorway.

Zara's room was magnificent. The room was painted in something that seemed to be blue mixed with silver. On the ceilings were navy butterflies, with wings flecked with gold that shimmered in the light, so they looked like they were flying. "I can't believe you live here," she finished, grinning. "It's the most wonderful thing I've ever seen." Zara rose her eyes slightly as she hopped onto her bed.

"I suppose it is pretty special," she answered, stretching her arms over her head as she yawned. "I guess you get used to it after a while."

"That's probably true, if it's all you know," Lottie agreed. She folded her arms as she looked around Zara's bedroom again. "For me, though... all the shimmering gold, the cronzaki, the unicorns... I'll never forget it, for as long as I live."

"What's Earth like?" Zara's excited question came quite suddenly. Lottie decided her new friend seemed much more outgoing and enthusiastic than she was.

"It's all right, I suppose," Lottie sighed eventually. "I mean, there's lots of great things about it," Lottie added, not wanting to downplay home. "We have nice blue skies like you do. Sometimes there are sunsets like yours, but it rains most of the time. Because the water is see-though," Lottie said, "when it rains it just goes kind of grey. It can look quite miserable sometimes."

"I see," Zara replied. "Sounds... very interesting." She sounded so deliberately polite it made them both crack up into giggles. "You've still got your mum, though, haven't you?" Zara added in a chortle. "Have you got a dad?"

"Yes, my dad is called Malcolm. Mum met him at uni." Zara frowned. "It's short for university," Lottie explained.

"It's a place of learning adults often go to on Earth, after they've finished school. I've got an older sister, too, called Nadia."

"I don't have any brothers or sisters," Zara commented, leaning her back against the wall. "My mum might've liked to have other children, maybe, but my dad died when I was little. I don't really remember him."

"I'm sorry," Lottie answered, her face creasing in sympathy. Zara only gave a little shrug and Lottie guessed her friend didn't want to talk about it any further. "Your mum is really nice," Lottie added quietly after a moment.

"Yeah, she is," Zara grinned again, her tone far brighter. "Come on, we better see what you might like to wear, before Mum wonders what's taking so long." With that she jumped to her feet and headed over to her wardrobe, quickly tugging the doors open. "What's your sister like?" Zara asked, her voice slightly muffled as she looked through her clothes.

"She's okay," Lottie answered a little reluctantly, giving a little shrug as she stood alone in the middle of Zara's bedroom. "She's twenty-three and doesn't live at home anymore, so I don't see her very much. She has her whole life and everything." Lottie stretched out her arms as she spoke, then let them fall limply to her sides again.

"We don't get on amazingly well, to be honest," Lottie admitted, as if suddenly remembering that her real life still existed. "I was a bit cross with my parents, because they made me stay at my aunt's creepy old house while they went to visit Nadia, even though it meant missing my birthday." Lottie frowned, hating how resentful and childish she sounded. "My sister is having problems with her job and her boyfriend, so they had to go see her."

"That does sound annoying," Zara empathised. "Although I guess if I was in trouble, I'd like Mum to come and help me." Lottie nodded, even though her new friend still had her head and shoulders ducked into her wardrobe. Zara had reminded her about what her dad had said, about trying to see things from other people's points of view.

"Would this work, do you think?" Zara suddenly straightened, outstretching her arms in Lottie's direction as she held out a dress to her.

"Oh, yes," Lottie breathed. "That will do very nicely." The dress was a faded lilac, a shade much more subtle and dignified than her bright purple dressing gown and fluffy socks. The dress then continued to gradually darken in colour, until it was almost black at the very bottom. Across the dress were sparkles of silver and gold, swirling in abstract patterns. Lottie thought wearing it would make her look like the night sky itself.

"Great!" Zara beamed excitedly. Lottie thought her new friend always seemed to be grinning. "I'll pop outside while you try it on." With that, Zara bounded out of the room. Lottie gazed at the beautiful dress a moment longer, before quickly peeling off her dressing gown. She noticed now that Zara had tactfully let out some underwear. Lottie quickly got changed, relishing in the soft feeling of her dress as she pulled it over her head. As she did so, she felt like she was stepping into the brand-new magical realm of Orovand all over again.

Lottie had always been more of a tomboy, favouring jeans and t-shirts rather than skirts and dresses. On this occasion, though, she decided it wasn't necessarily a bad thing to feel like a princess sometimes. She gave into the temptation of lifting her arms and giving a bit of a twirl.

"Can I come in yet?" came Zara's impatient voice. Lottie giggled and told her yes, impressed Zara waited for an answer before just striding back into her bedroom. "Wow! You look amazing, Lottie!" Zara told her.

"Thanks." Lottie grinned shyly. Over the next few minutes, while Zara gave her different shoes to try on, the two chattered away on what Earth was like. Lottie hadn't expected her new friend to ask so many questions or be so interested in the answers. It made Lottie think that maybe life on Earth wasn't so bad after all. Maybe one could even have adventures back home, too, possibly even when staying in creepy old barn in rural Yorkshire.

"There," Zara said in triumph, as Lottie finally found a pair of shoes that seemed to fit her well. They were silver and white, somehow both complementing and contrasting with the dress at the same time. Just as Lottie stood to survey herself in the crystal mirror in the corner of the bedroom, there came a knock at the door.

"Hi, girls, how's it going?" Guira opened the door. "I just came to see... oh, Lottie, how wonderful you look," Zara's mum said kindly. "That's the dress Zara wore to Prince Andri's birthday party last month." Guira nodded, smiling with approval. "It does suit a royal occasion more than pyjamas," she added with a wink.

"Yeah, probably," Lottie replied with a grin. She took a deep breath, feeling rather wonderful as she twirled again. The break in Zara's room seemed to have done her a lot of good. "I think I'm ready to meet King Karalius," Lottie said definitively.

"Excellent. He's heard you've arrived and is most looking forward to meeting you. Shall we head back to the palace?"

she suggested, her arm gesturing out of the door as she spoke. The three of them left Zara's bedroom and as they emerged back out into the corridor, Lottie felt some of her new-found confidence threaten to fade away. As they descended the grand staircase again, Lottie swallowed hard, battling against her resurfacing shyness.

They went back to the grand hall, then turned right which led to a corridor far more ornately decorated than the ones upstairs. The paintings seemed far more majestic, with blue men and women wearing crowns—Lottie guessed they were previous kings and queens of Orovand, but really, she was so preoccupied with meeting King Karalius, she wasn't giving them much thought.

"Well, I'll go tell the king you're outside," Guira said as they came to a stop outside the door, where the burgundy carpet seemed even more plush and exquisite. "I'll just go in first to announce you. Zara, why don't you brief Lottie on what to do?" Zara nodded, while Lottie's gaze fell. Right here outside the king's throne room, her courage was starting to fail.

"No need to fret, dear," Guira encouraged kindly, noticing Lottie's nervousness. "I'm sure you'll do brilliantly," she added, laying a hand briefly on Lottie's shoulder. Lottie wanted to thank her, but suddenly her throat was far too tight, so she only nodded. Guira gave her a final smile and nod, before the guard outside admitted her into the throne room.

"You just give a big bow when you walk in," Zara began, as the door closed in front of them, before she demonstrated by bowing low. "Then you slowly approach the throne, looking down at the floor. When you get near, you look up, address him as 'Your Majesty' and bow again." Suddenly, Zara stifled a yawn and Lottie's eyes widened. Could her new friend be bored? Then again, Lottie realised, Zara had probably done this countless times, if her mum was one of the king's advisors.

"Then you don't speak to him again, unless you're spoken to. Which you probably will," Zara added with a grin, "because you're the first human visitor to come in a century, you're kind of interesting." Lottie gave a quick smile at this. "Keep calling him 'Your Majesty' like with every sentence," Zara continued.

"Stand there until he's finished talking and he dismisses you, then you bow again and walk backwards for ten steps before you turn to leave." Zara concluded, then stopped to frown a minute. "Yep, I think that's it. You ok?" she added to Lottie.

"Uh, yeah, I think so." Lottie tried to smile, trying to sound confident. Her hands lowered to once again self-consciously straighten her dress. Lottie took a deep breath, then, taking her final moment to prepare herself for meeting the King of Orovand.

"You'll do great," Zara whispered, as Lottie heard her name being announced. The grand ornate doors swung open to admit her. Lottie took a nervous step forwards and bowed low, hoping she had done it just as Zara had shown her. The two girls then slowly approached the throne. As Lottie kept her head down, she slyly glanced to Zara's feet to keep the same pace as her.

"Your Majesty," Lottie greeted him as respectfully as she could, while at the same trying not to let her voice tremble. After she spoke, she lifted her head, finally daring to look at him. King Karalius was blue, the same as every other person here, except his dark hair and beard had streaks of grey running through it. He was the first person she had met in the Gold Dimension that could be described as 'old'. Lottie had no idea how long people lived in Orovand, so she didn't know whether the king was seventy or three hundred.

"Ah, Lottie Armitage, at last. Guira's told me all about you." His eyes crinkled when he smiled, the same way her Aunt Susan's did. Lottie hoped this meant he was as kind a king as Zara had told her.

Then Lottie realised King Karalius hadn't said anything further and fought not to panic. He had spoken to her, but it hadn't been a question. Should she say something? She was desperate to look to Guira or Zara for help, but she didn't want to disrespect the king by looking away from him. Lottie tried to give a small, respectful smile, fighting the urge to bite her lip.

"Welcome to the Kingdom of Oruvesi, Lottie Armitage, in the realm of Orovand," King Karalius declared formally, his booming voice echoing off the throne room walls. Lottie had never been so relieved as to hear someone speak. "Tell me, Lottie, are you enjoying your stay with us so far?" He asked her, his tone gentle.

"Yes, Your Majesty, very much," Lottie replied, as bravely as she could, even more relieved to know she should speak, given he had asked her a question. Guira gave her an encouraging smile.

"It's most wonderful to have you here, Lottie." King Karalius' deep voice still echoed a little around the palace hall. "We haven't had a human being come here to these lands since Julie Sawyer. Guira tells me you are her daughter?"

"Yes, Your Majesty," Lottie answered. The king paused again. Lottie swallowed her dry throat, waiting. Absently she reflected how Zara hadn't said a word, but this didn't seem to bother her new friend.

"Well, Lottie, it is an honour to meet you. I look forward to seeing you at the ceremony later." Then the king smiled. Lottie inclined her head a little, but inside she was fighting not to panic. His tone had been dismissive, should she leave now, or would he say something official? Then King Karalius came to her rescue again, as he nodded to Guira. "Thank you, that will be all for now."

"Yes, Your Majesty," Guira bowed to him, then glanced to Lottie and nodded. King Karalius looked her way again.

"Your Majesty," Lottie repeated his title as she bowed low again. The three of them walked backwards, until right next to the door, then she turned to follow Guira out of the throne room.

"Well done, Lottie," Guira said, clapping her hand on Lottie's shoulder again as she smiled. "You did splendidly."

"Thanks." Lottie breathed in relief. "He was very kind to me." She stood there in the middle of the corridor, smiling a little.

"We have almost three hours before the ceremony," Guira said now. "I think it would be a good idea for you to get some rest before then."

"I'm..." Lottie started to object, but then suddenly realised how tired she was. She remembered, too, that it was past midnight when she'd left Earth. "That would be good, actually," she admitted.

"Wow, you must be really tired," Zara said, eyes wide. Lottie grinned, guessing from her friend's comment that it was not an easy operation for Guira to get her daughter to go to bed.

"There's a spare room in the palace you can stay in, near to Zara's bedroom. Come on." Stifling a yawn with her hand, Lottie followed Guira back up to the staircase with the red carpet. Indeed, the closer they got to the spare room, the more exhausted Lottie became. They stopped at Zara's room first, so they could pick up her pyjamas, dressing gown and socks. Then Guira and Zara took her to the spare room and left her to it, with Zara promising to come and wake her up later.

As much as Lottie loved Zara's dress, she found it was quite a relief to change back into her pyjamas and crawl into the bed, which was very comfortable. The girl's last thought was how she could ever sleep with all her magical experiences racing through her mind. Then, though, all the excitement of the day caught up with her so that really, Lottie's head had barely touched the pillow before she fell deeply asleep.

Chapter Five

"Lottie?" Lottie opened her eyes to hear Zara calling to her, while knocking on the door very loudly. "Sorry to wake you, but the ceremony will start soon."

"Okay," she mumbled sleepily, then suddenly sat up in bed, completely alert. With wide eyes, Lottie slowly took in the surroundings of the spare room. "It wasn't a dream," she whispered to herself. She realised until now, part of her had been wondering if she had been dreaming still, but surely, she would have woken up at home. The fact she'd woken up still in Orovand meant it was real, didn't it?

"You can come in, if you like," Lottie called, rubbing her eyes as she talked. Zara needed no further invitation as she bounded into the room, a cup of gold water in one hand.

"Hi," Zara said and grinned. Lottie wondered absently for a moment if her blue friend ever got tired. Maybe people from Orovand didn't need as much sleep, or maybe Zara was just a particularly energetic twelve-year-old. "Did you get some rest?"

"Yeah, I feel a bit better, actually." Lottie hopped out of bed. The dress that reminded her of the night sky was hung neatly over a chair where she'd left it. "How long have we got?"

"About an hour, Mum said," Zara answered. "Oh, you still have a bit of your cronzaki left if you're hungry. I would've eaten it all by now," she added, beaming. Lottie grinned back as she took another bite, then she frowned.

"My mouth's gone all salty now," she said, "but it's so delicious!" The taste slid wonderfully over her tongue once more. Zara giggled, nodding.

"Yeah, that's the only downside to them. It's special salt from Orovand, it comes all the way from the Mavi Mountains," Zara explained, bursting with pride. "Dendari is from the mountains, I think, so he's an expert in using it in baking."

"Do people still live in the mountains now?" Lottie asked thoughtfully as she tore off another delicious chunk of cronzaki with her teeth to pop in her mouth.

"No, I don't think so," Zara shook her head. "Well, I mean, there might be a couple of villages left. There used to be a few towns, but nobody's lived there for years," she continued, shrugging. "Almost everyone lives in one of the cities by now. Some of the people left there don't like that, I think… I think it's affected their trade or something, I don't know. It's something my mum told me once." Lottie's new friend shrugged again.

"Anyway, that's why I got you some water. They don't taste that salty at the time, but it really kicks in afterwards. Here," she added, holding up the cup as Lottie finished her last mouthful of the heavenly snack, leaving the wrapper crumpled in her dressing gown pocket.

"Thanks." Lottie smiled and took a drink of the water. The strange mix of strong mineral water with the sweet honey-like taste at once entered her mouth, but she found she was more used to the different taste now. Absently, Lottie wondered how she might find the taste of Earth's water once she got back home. "So, do lots of people go to the ceremony?" Lottie asked, between sips.

"Oh, yeah," Zara answered. "Everyone at court comes to the ceremony. It takes place at the cave where we found you earlier." Lottie nodded, remembering they had said to Preto, the man at the cave guarding the lockets, that they would see him that evening.

"King Karalius and all the important people get to be in the cave itself," Zara continued. "I get to be there because of Mum. That's why we were there earlier," she added. "It's one of Mum's jobs to check with Preto that the lockets appeared safely. I don't know what we'd do if they didn't," she said then, thinking aloud. "We weren't expecting you, of course," Zara said and grinned.

"I wasn't expecting to be there, either," Lottie returned drily as she drank more of the water. Absently, she wiped a drop at the side of her mouth, but it was almost dry again, like in the cave.

"That's true," Zara giggled, then stretched her arms over her head. "I think mum is expecting us downstairs soon. I'll go wait outside again."

"Okay," Lottie nodded. "I'll see you in a minute." As soon as Zara closed the door behind her, the girl quickly changed into the dress again. There was a spare brush on the bedside table, so Lottie ran it through her hair a few times before putting it back in a ponytail. Lottie left her pyjamas and dressing gown folded on the bed, assuming she would probably be back here later. She had no idea how long Preto would need her locket for. Besides, Lottie was finding herself in less and less of a rush to leave.

***

Lottie kept glancing at the lockets, but nothing had happened yet. They were stood in the cave, near to the pool where she had appeared a few hours earlier. Lottie was pleased that only the officials were in the cave for the ceremony itself, as that had been overwhelming enough. King Karalius had announced Lottie almost as soon as they got to the cave, which suddenly meant she had been lost in a sea of blue people queueing up to meet her, wanting to shake her hand. Lottie had lost count of the people who had told her that their parents or grandparents had met her mother.

It meant Lottie was extremely relieved now the ceremony had officially started. Most of it was King Karalius' voice booming through the cave. In the palace hall she had found his loudness jarring, but here it was comforting. For as long as he carried on talking, she felt safe, because if he was speaking, people couldn't talk to her!

A few minutes later, though, King Karalius announced that there would be a pause before the part everyone was waiting for—when the lockets would form a link to Earth and power up the gold in Orovand. Almost as soon as he'd finished speaking, yet more people looked to her. Some began walking towards her and in the few moments before they reached her, Lottie braced herself.

"Hey Lottie," Zara said quickly, deliberately stepping in front of Lottie. Out of the corner of her eye, Lottie saw people stop, while still looking at her with interest. "I'd like to introduce you to Prince Andriana," she swept her arm grandly. "We just call him Andri," she added, winking as she straightened. Then, suddenly, King Karalius' son and heir, was stood in front of her too. He was a fair bit taller than Zara and Lottie suspected he was a few years older than them.

"Your Highness," Lottie greeted, bowing her head a little rather than going for the full-on, almost reaching for your toes bow she had given his father. She saw Prince Andri had the same short, pointed nose and thick eyebrows as his father and his blue chin was peppered with stubble. He was smiling at her with the same kind eyes as King Karalius, too.

"Nice to meet you, Lottie," Andri said, grinning as he reached out his hand. "I bet you're finding meeting everyone a bit overwhelming," he added, as she shook it. Lottie then realised Zara had deliberately introduced the prince to her, to stop the masses who wanted to meet her.

"Just a little," Lottie admitted with a smile, immensely grateful for her friend's tact, that she only had to meet one new person rather than yet more masses of interested strangers.

"I'm sure people on Earth would react the same if one of you magically showed up," she said, feeling a little braver. Andri grinned. The three of them talked easily for a while, before Zara suddenly pointed.

"Look!" Zara whispered loudly, just as a collective silence fell over the crowd. Lottie immediately turned her gaze to the cave wall. Her eyes widened as the lockets began to glow, realising it was the same kind of shining her locket had done back in the bathroom of Aunt Susan's house. Only now it wasn't just her locket—all fifty lockets were gleaming brightly together.

As Lottie watched, utterly mesmerised, the lockets glowed brighter and brighter, until there was a sea of golden flames embracing the magical jewellery. Just as the burning blaze of gold reached its peak, like a sunset back on earth,

Preto drew his sword. He held it suspended into the air a moment, before driving it into a silver pedestal upon the ground.

One by one, the lockets flew from the hooks on the cave wall. They floated into position in a large circle, hovering above the silver pedestal. The glow of the lockets morphed, then, leaving the lockets to form a huge, dazzling golden ball in the middle of the circle that the lockets created.

"That's the power the lockets create," Zara whispered in Lottie's ear. The ball kept burning brighter, until it was almost blinding. Then, suddenly, the huge golden sphere, looking as fierce and volatile as the sun, shot out of the mouth of the cavern. Lottie, stood near the cave's entrance, turned and craned her neck for a better view. The golden ball rose high up into the air, swiftly vanishing out of sight as the orb soared above the turquoise forest.

"Come on," Zara murmured, tugging at Lottie's wrist. "We'll miss it otherwise. It's the best bit!" The two girls joined the throng of officials leaving the cavern. Leading this procession very regally was King Karalius. Lottie noticed Prince Andri was now standing beside his father.

As they stood free of the cave out in the forest air, Lottie saw it looked like thousands of people had gathered outside, clamouring together to see the dazzling golden orb. She guessed it was most of the city, but she had no idea how big the population of Oruvesi was. As Lottie looked at the people, she saw the flecks of gold on their skin were glowing, pulsating in a kind of rhythm with the golden ball.

"Look!" Zara nearly shrieked in her ear, pointing. Lottie turned her gaze skyward. The orb was much bigger and nearly hurt to look at; it really was like the sun was several feet above

74

her, casting everything it touched in light and warmth. The ball grew larger than ever, ready to burst.

Then, abruptly, the orb full of golden light exploded. Lottie gasped, the whole of her breath leaving her body. Gold streams forked and streaked across the sky like lightning, with bolts crashing and ricocheting off each other, casting particles of gold in their wake, in every direction. It was like a storm of dazzling fireworks.

"Wow!" Lottie gasped again, struck in wonder by the fantastic display. The lightning continued until at last every streak had ended. The whole sky was left shimmering with ten thousand golden stars, each as flittering and beautiful as the last.

"Some of the golden light will remain in the sky, mixing with the clouds," Guira said quietly, making Lottie jump a little. The people of Orovand were beginning to murmur to one another now, talking excitedly about the ceremony that would, for another year, power everything in their world.

"That will produce the gold rain, to help the water keep its levels of purity," Guira continued to explain. Lottie listened as she watched the glittering sky above, amazed at the beautiful process she had just witnessed. "The rest of the particles will fall to the earth," Guira added now. "It will help our crops to grow and keep our buildings safe."

"You can see it start now, look," Zara marvelled. As Lottie gazed at the sky, she saw they were right. Whilst the higher layers of gold particles were rising further to clouds, the lower shimmering specks were already gently descending to the land. Lottie watched the people extend their hands to the sky, smiling gratefully as the power of their world floated down all around them. Lottie then copied them, raising her own arms.

She glanced to her hands to see several tiny specks of gold landing on them, glowing on their skin briefly before disappearing.

"No wonder it's called the Gold Dimension," Lottie muttered to herself. Zara giggled. "I'm absorbing it," she added, looking to her hands. "That might be how my mum first got it into her bloodstream, if she watched the ceremony."

"That's one theory, yes," Guira agreed, nodding. "There must have been gold in her blood before then, though, for her to come to Orovand in the first place. If all the human visitors who have ever come to Orovand are genetically linked, there must be one ancestor who started it all," Guira speculated, folding her arms now as she thought.

"I wonder how the first human got here," Zara murmured aloud, still watching the golden flecks fall from the sky, like snow in sunset. Lottie didn't have an answer to that—it seemed no one else in Orovand knew either. So instead they simply watched quietly for a few moments, till at last the gold particles had either fallen to the ground, or faded into the clouds. Lottie knew that even after the last fleck disappeared the power would remain, tangibly channelling into their world.

In the wake of the final gold flakes vanishing, the crowd began to leave, making their way as one down the forest path, the same way Lottie had walked to Oruvesi with Guira and Zara earlier.

"Can we go to the feast now, Mum, please?" Zara asked a little too loudly, stretching her arms above her head. Lottie got from her friend's excitement that she was probably very hungry.

"Come on, then," Guira smirked, slipping arm around her daughter's shoulder. "Our carriage awaits," she added, sweeping grandly with her free arm towards the carriage in question. As the three of them walked over, Lottie found she still couldn't take her eyes off the unicorns next to the carriage. They were the same beautiful creatures Lottie had met outside the palace and Lottie thought they looked just as majestic as ever.

"Ready whenever you are, Karoc," Guira called, after they had clambered into the carriage, door safely shut behind them. "Well, Lottie," Guira said. "What did you think?"

"It was..." Lottie paused as she swallowed, hardly able to find the words to describe what she had just witnessed. "It was so wonderful," Lottie said, knowing the word didn't do what she had experienced justice. "It was so moving, too. I feel like..." her voice trailed away again as she thought. "Like I really witnessed the heart of your people and what Orovand is about," she continued, a little frown of concentration on her face, looking to one of the plush carriage cushions as she spoke.

"It's made me understand more your world a bit more and how important gold is, for everything here," Lottie concluded. Then, feeling a little self-conscious, she fell quiet again.

"That's beautifully put, Lottie," Guira replied gently. Lottie wasn't sure, but she wondered if Zara's mum sounded a bit emotional. Neither of them said anything further. Zara was being unusually quiet, too, but when Lottie glanced at her, she saw Zara's head was craned out of the window, looking to the sky. Lottie wondered if her friend was desperate to try to see any remaining flecks of gold falling, but they had all faded by now.

Lottie sat back then for a few minutes, relieved that there were no longer hundreds of people lining up to meet her. She enjoyed the relative quiet, listening to the steady clopping of the horses—no, not horses, unicorns, she remembered excitedly—and the gentle way the carriage rocked them as they rode back to the city.

The carriage rode them back down the main roads of Oruvesi, then turned onto the luxurious circle of road outside the palace. Karoc drew them to a stop outside the steps and Lottie hopped out. Immediately, she swivelled around, desperate to get another look at the marvellous unicorns. They were looking at the carriage driver intently as he fed them with handfuls of what seemed to be oats, or Orovand's equivalent to oats, anyway.

Then, turning to see that Guira and Zara were ready to head into the palace, Lottie gave them a shaky smile to hide her nerves. The carriage ride had been a bit of a break, but now Lottie would have to meet lots more people at the feast. She swallowed, knowing her dry mouth wasn't just due to her nerves.

"I can still taste the salt from the cronzaki, is that normal?" Lottie asked Zara in a low voice. Zara glanced to her, nodding as they went up the steps to the grand entrance hall.

"Yeah, that's the Orovand salt still, it lingers around for a while, but it means you are kept fuller for longer, apparently," Zara added with a shrug. "Or so Mum says." The two of them walked behind Guira down yet another corridor. This one was lined with plush burgundy carpet.

"Don't worry, the feast will start in a minute," Zara told her, while Lottie looked around. "You can get a drink then."

"Okay, thanks," Lottie murmured. To her left and right, yet more portraits of noble people hung on the walls. In fact, it was only slightly less exquisite than the corridor that had led to King Karalius' throne room.

If she was honest, Lottie wasn't just looking at all the paintings because she was interested. She was again fighting her nerves, resisting hard the temptation to start biting her lip. In that moment, Lottie wished she could be as confident, bounding about like Zara did. Deep down, Lottie knew it wasn't just because she was in a brand-new world that she was nervous. Somehow, she knew that if it was the other way around and Lottie was showing Zara her world, then her new friend would still probably be more confident back home than she herself had ever been on Earth.

"Here we are," Guira said, taking Lottie out of her own thoughts a bit, as Lottie and Zara followed her through the big doors at the other end of the corridor to a room even bigger than the grand entrance hall. Six long tables were laid in two rows of three, each one almost the length of the entire banquet hall. Ten chairs lined up neatly on either side of each table.

"Wow," Lottie murmured, her eyes full of the scene. The decoration of the tables was resplendent, with gold and crystal crockery reflecting onto delicate table coverings, which were in regal hues of red and purple. Every chair was covered with a plush silver cover, which gleamed as pure and as fathomless as moonlight. All the reflection came from the large chandeliers suspended from the ceiling, with small flames emitting from each hanging crystal shard.

Looking closer at the tables, Lottie saw each seating place was well spread out along the table, with a large plate and a much smaller plate. Elegant cutlery was set out beside the ornate crockery. At least they seemed to be rather ordinary-looking knives and forks, but there were so many and she had absolutely no clue what she should use when.

"Don't worry," Zara murmured, still stood beside Lottie, as if she could read her mind. "I'll show you what to use and when," Lottie only nodded.

"It is a pleasure to meet you at last, Lottie Armitage from Earth." Lottie turned at the deep, welcoming voice, to see it was Preto who had spoken. This close, he looked huger than ever. His dark, raspberry jam dreadlocks swayed loosely about his shoulders as he bent his head to her.

"I… thank you. An honour to meet you, as well," Lottie managed, almost lost as she looked up to his face. After a while, conversation with this citizen from Orovand would certainly give her a crick in her neck. Preto bowed his head again.

"I wished to return this to you at the earliest convenience, daughter of Julie Sawyer." He held out his hand to her. Lottie looked down to see her locket was nestled safely in his palm.

"Oh, thank you," Lottie stammered, as she reached to take it from him. Preto did not speak further, but merely bent his head a final time before moving away, as quickly as he'd appeared.

"Wow, even Preto's talked to you!" Zara muttered. Lottie nearly jumped—she'd been so engrossed in watching the Guardian of the Lockets walking away, she had almost forgotten her new friend was still stood beside her. "He hardly talks to anyone," Zara continued, then smiled. "I'm glad you got your locket back, anyway.

"Yeah." Lottie smiled happily. Lottie couldn't quite explain it, but she'd felt a lot better the moment she'd taken her locket back from Preto. There was an innate rightness about it, as if Lottie truly knew that the locket belonged with her and that she, in turn, belonged with her locket.

"There were fifty of them, right?" Lottie commented, holding up her locket to inspect it. Somehow, she knew that she had her locket back rather than any of the others, but how did Preto know? They were all almost identical.

"You're wondering how he knew which one was yours?" Zara guessed, grinning. "I suppose if my whole job was taking care of them while they were in Orovand, I'd be able to tell them apart, too. Do you want me to help you put it on?" She offered kindly.

"Sure, thanks," Lottie answered, slipping the locket around the front of her neck. She then turned around and Zara stepped forwards, taking the two ends of the chain from her.

"All done," Zara said, stepping back again. As Lottie turned back around, feeling the small weight of the locket hanging just at the top of her chest, something began to change. Her nerves didn't disappear completely, but the butterflies in her stomach certainly settled a bit. Wearing her locket in Orovand made a kind of peace start to lap around her body, giving a contentment beyond her anxieties. At once Lottie wondered how, if her mother had the same sensation at wearing the locket, she had ever been able to pass it on to her.

"Here, you can sit next to me," Zara suggested. Smiling, Lottie followed Zara through to some chairs near the top end of the table in the middle of the hall, grateful she could sit next to her friend. The plates had gold twine wrapped delicately around the edges, almost making them look like wreaths at Christmas.

Beside the plates was a crystal goblet, but it was empty. Lottie didn't mind not eating yet, but she was desperate for a drink. There was a crystal decanter not far away filled with water, but nobody else seemed to be touching it. It might be they had to wait for the feast to begin.

Absently, Lottie began to wonder who might be sat on the other side to her. Even with the confidence of her locket and the night-sky dress Lottie felt the ball of anxiety growing again. She chewed the inside of her bottom lip as she shifted on the luxurious chair, again setting her determination to try to enjoy the evening if she could.

"Here we are then," Guira stated brightly again and the corner of Lottie's mouth twitched. Each time Guira said something like that, it reminded her of her own mother. She usually found it irritating when her mum said it, but Lottie found it comforting, as if something of Julie Armitage was with her still, even in this strange new world. It gave her hope too, to know that her mum would have done all this before, paving the way for her to do it also.

Guira moved to take her seat on the other side of Lottie. Lottie smiled fully, feeling more tension seep away from her shoulders at the tact of her new friends. No matter who might sit opposite her, she could always talk to them.

In the end, Guira was only sat down for a few seconds before suddenly she and Zara had leapt to their feet, along with everyone else in the grand banquet hall. Only a moment later, Lottie jumped up to follow suit.

Chapter Six

"His Majesty King Karalius, His Royal Highness Prince Andriana," a tall noble with a black-and-gold moustache announced, gesturing regally from the corner of the room. The king and the prince walked regally across the hall, the light from the chandeliers making their royal robes gleam, softly flickering their blue and gold skin. King Karalius still wore his crown from the ceremony; a sheen of vivid gold with red rubies dotted all around.

"Please take a seat," the King of Orovand instructed. As one, Lottie and the rest of his royal officials and guests quickly sat back down on the plush chairs.

"We gather here today," King Karalius began, "in celebration of the power of the lockets. We know that they will forever form the link between the Gold Dimension and Earth." At this Lottie sat back a little in her chair, settling in for another long speech from the king. Not that she minded—in fact she rather enjoyed them.

"We are especially privileged to have at our table Lottie Armitage, daughter of Julie Sawyer." Lottie only had a fraction of a second to ready herself for every head turning to hers.

"Stand up, Lottie," Guira whispered on the other side of her. Lottie stood so quickly, she almost knocked her plate.

"Welcome, Lottie," he greeted. There was a moment where Lottie fought her panic, trying to decide whether she should say something. He was addressing her directly, so she risked it.

"Thank you for your kind welcome, Your Majesty," Lottie answered with all the braveness she didn't really feel, bending her head low, in what she hoped was a respectful enough bow. "It truly is an honour to be here among the people of Orovand."

"Excellent," King Karalius beamed, seeming pleased with her answer. "Of course, we all know the importance of gold to our lives," he added, turning his attention back to the rest of his court and noble guests. "The history and tradition of this ceremony…"

"Well done," Guira whispered as Lottie sat down again, relieved that King Karalius was continuing his speech, "That was perfect." Lottie only gave a little nod, thankful that her time in the spotlight was again over. Lottie had already fallen in love with the magical world of Orovand, but she had always hated being the centre of attention. As Lottie listened to King Karalius, she wriggled her tongue round in her mouth, trying to swallow again. If anything, it was like the taste of the salt was getting stronger. She guessed that everyone else in Orovand must just be used to it.

"Let the feast begin!" King Karalius finally announced a few minutes later, waving a hand and taking a seat himself onto a chair that was twice as grand as all the others. An instant later and lines of servants suddenly appeared from the kitchen, bearing silver trays. Lottie began to relax further, wondering what the food might be like here. Would it be similar to meals on Earth?

"Here, Lottie," Guira said warmly, "let's get you a drink." At last, she was poured the gold water. Lottie quickly reached for it and took a sip, before realising it wasn't like the water in the cave. Up close, she saw there was a greenish tinge to it. It tasted wonderfully familiar, though, so Lottie took several swift gulps, deliciously quenching her thirst.

"You like it?" asked Zara, on the other side to her. "It's made specially from our apples," she explained. "There's an orchard just outside Oruvesi."

"Ah, of course! We make juice from apples, too." Now Zara had said it, that sweet, crisp tang was obvious. There were other flavours mixed in, too, that had disguised the taste of the apples. There was a warm spice and a shot of something slightly sharp that took the edge of the sweetness.

"It's wonderful," Lottie commented, taking another drink of the refreshing, golden-green juice that at last seemed to remove the flavour of salt in her mouth. If she wasn't careful, Lottie knew she could probably drain the whole crystal jug just by herself, when it was obviously also meant for others sat nearby. Deliberately, she set her goblet down back on the table, just as a servant put down a bowl of what looked like soup on her plate, except the liquid was black, with silver flecks.

"The big spoon on your left," Zara whispered with a wink. Lottie grinned and picked up the right implement, just as a delicious whiff from whatever was in the bowl reached her nostrils.

In the end, the feast was similar enough to the food Lottie knew from Earth, yet each flavour was somehow different from anything she'd experienced before. The black soup seemed to taste strongly of mushrooms, which fortunately Lottie loved. It was mixed with a flavour that could have been something like pork, but she couldn't be sure.

"Who's that?" Lottie muttered to Guira, after she had swallowed another mouthful of the delicious soup. She nodded to a man in the middle of the table in front of her, on the left-hand side of the room. He had a cape almost as ornate as the king's and wore a little crown of his own. "He looks very important," Lottie commented.

"Yes, his name is Lord Jakad," Guira informed her. "He is the ruler of Tilajin, our city to the south. He has a very good friendship with King Karalius."

"I've met him a couple of times, he's nice," Zara chimed in, on the other side of her. "I've met his maid, Taranai, too. That's her now," she added, just as a young lady, looking about eighteen or so, refilled Lord Jakad's goblet with more of the Gold Dimension's version of apple juice. "Lots of the officials have servants," Zara now explained.

Lottie nodded, trying to understand more and more of Orovand with everything Guira and Zara said. Every table seemed to be filled with officials and nobles, members of King Karalius' court in some way. As the servants came to clear the soup bowls, Lottie tried to imagine what it would be like to live here every day in this wonderful world, let alone in this luxurious palace.

A few minutes later, dishes were placed on top of the large plates that looked more recognisable. It seemed to be meat and vegetables, covered with a thick, creamy sauce. Even the tongs were ornate, as servants put fresh, round rolls onto each side plate. The scent of the bread was heavenly.

After Zara showed her which cutlery to use, Lottie dug in with relish. The roll was sweeter than the bread she knew from back on Earth, melting in her mouth. It was almost like desert, but then when she copied Guira and Zara, dipping the bread into the sauce, she understood. For the creamy gravy was slightly too strong to properly enjoy on its own, but combined with the bread, it was the perfect combination of savoury and sweet. It left her squashing the urge to eat all the bread and gravy at once.

Eagerly, though, Lottie turned her attention to the other elements of her meal. The meat itself was something like roast chicken, but somehow, with the lingering flavour of unsweetened almonds. Beneath the meat were small black grains of what could be rice, only far crunchier and with the kick of something spicy. The mix of the flavours together, Lottie decided, made for one of the best meals she had ever eaten.

Halfway through dinner, the servants came around again, silver trays laden with more of those sweet, delicious rolls. Lottie eagerly accepted another. She hadn't realised how hungry she had become, even with having the cronzaki this afternoon. Lottie frowned, thinking how if she was on Earth, probably around now she would be waking up for breakfast, but she was never usually so ravenous for the first meal of the day. Maybe it was the excitement of the last few hours, or perhaps she had used up a lot of energy when the locket transported her here. Either way, Lottie was delighted to have so much room in her stomach to try everything.

"The rolls are great, aren't they?" Zara reached for another one as she spoke, her mouth half full still. Lottie giggled, nodding as she took another drink of the wonderful spiced apple juice. Guira turned to her, simply raising an eyebrow at the somewhat undignified way her daughter was eating. Zara noticed at once and swallowed before smiling rather reproachfully.

"Sorry, Mum," Zara quickly said, without really feeling that remorseful. Then she suddenly hiccupped loudly and clapped her hand over her mouth, eyes wide with embarrassment as others looked her way. Lottie pursed her lips at once, trying her best not to succumb to giggles at her friend's unfortunate timing.

"I see you are enjoying yourself, young Zara," came the gravelly voice of King Karalius. Lottie pressed her lips together harder. "Perhaps some more juice? I find hydration is a useful ally against hiccups." His eyes were dancing with humour as he spoke. At once, everyone else began to laugh and Lottie at last dissolved into giggles. Zara only grinned, bending her head low towards the king.

"An excellent idea, Your Majesty," Zara agreed easily. She then grabbed the jug to pour herself some more juice, taking a moment to collect herself before taking a sip.

"Take your time with your food, daughter," Guira rebuked now, though a small smile was now across her own features.

"Of course, Mother," Zara agreed easily. She picked up her napkin and delicately dabbed at the corners of her mouth. She was now trying to look so refined that everyone, including her mother, chuckled again. Then, suddenly, Lottie noticed then that everyone on this half of the table was smiling at Zara, even King Karalius. More importantly, Zara didn't seem to mind at all.

That thought stayed with Lottie throughout the rest of dinner, reflecting on how bubbly and outgoing Zara was. Then suddenly the feast was over, with the servants collecting the rest of the plates. The last course had been something like cheese, but Lottie had only really nibbled at it.

Everyone was getting up and moving around the tables to mingle. It was what Lottie dreaded, because just like in the cave, people were coming up to her from all directions, shaking her hand, asking questions about Earth.

Lottie smiled politely, told them how much she was enjoying Orovand and answered their questions about life back home as best she could. All the while, though, Lottie was getting more and more drained. Once or twice she caught a glimpse of Zara, still stood relatively close, but chatting easily to the officials as if she'd done it all her life. Then Lottie realised Zara had mingled with nobles since she was small, if her mum had always worked at the palace.

Lottie knew that even if she'd lived in the Gold Dimension all her life, she still would hate all the attention. Lottie knew, then, how different she was to Zara. It wasn't because her skin was white, rather than blue flecked with gold. Her new friend was infinitely more comfortable and confident here than Lottie had ever been on Earth.

The servants were weaving in and out of the nobles, balancing trays of the apple juice and handing out what Lottie recognised as cronzakis, only this time they were miniature. She remembered what Guira had said about Dendari baking things for the end of the feast.

"It's getting a bit warm in here, isn't it?" Zara was next to Lottie, covering her mouth while she yawned. "Fancy taking a break outside?"

"Sure," Lottie replied, trying to sound neutral. On the inside she was leaping with relief at the thought of escaping the reams of officials. The girls sneakily made their way out of the hall, only pausing to get a fresh cup of apple juice and cronzaki on the way out.

"Much better out here," Zara commented, as they came to a low wall directly facing the palace gardens. Lottie nodded. She could glimpse the shapes of hedges in the distance, but she couldn't fully make them out in the darkness. Zara hopped onto the wall, swishing her dangling legs gently. Lottie remained where she was, taking a small sip of the juice.

"Hey, you ok?" Zara's voice came abruptly, far softer than she expected. Lottie gave another nod. Ridiculously, she felt close to tears. "It must be a lot to take in," her new friend added quietly.

"It's not just that." Lottie tried desperately to keep her voice even, to not let her friend know how upset she was. "I just get sad sometimes that…" Lottie paused, feeling listless. "I've never been very good at talking to new people," Lottie resumed. "I don't have that many friends," she finally concluded, staring in the dark down to her untouched cronzaki.

"Really?" Zara sounded shocked. "But you're so nice!" she protested. At this, Lottie managed a small smile.

"Thanks. Mum says I've always been really quiet," Lottie said. Her voice was faraway, as if she was now talking to herself more than to Zara. "At school, everyone seems so noisy and runs around the playground and I… I just tend to walk round by myself." She sniffed here, bowing her head so Zara wouldn't see any of the tears that threatened to fall.

"I hate feeling like this!" she burst out angrily, sniffing again. "The other kids in my class think I'm unfriendly, but I'm just…shy," she finished quickly, before her voice caught.

"That sounds hard," Zara commented, the sympathy in her voice clear. Lottie was glad her new friend was just listening, rather than giving her loads of advice about how to change or deal with it better. "It must be difficult, then, being in a strange new world, meeting all these different people," Zara said now.

"Yeah, that's not been the most fun, I'll admit," Lottie admitted wryly, a smile threatening to return as she spoke.

Lottie sniffed, raising a hand to wipe away the few tears that had fallen.

"I don't know what school is like in Orovand," Lottie said now, "but on Earth, you go to a new school when you're eleven. I only have a few months left before I go to this big new school, with lots of new students I won't know." She sniffed a third time. "I'm scared I won't have any friends there, either. I wish I could be more like you," Lottie added, glancing to Zara. She saw her new friend's eyes widen in surprise, but still her friend just sat quietly in the dark, listening.

"I was watching you, earlier," Lottie explained, looking down at the pretty shoes Zara had lent her. "When you were talking to people at dinner you seemed so confident and comfortable. Even when you hiccupped," Lottie added, her lips twitching at the memory. "I would've been really embarrassed," she added, the smile fading again. "You weren't bothered at all, though. I wish I could be more like that," she concluded a little sadly.

"Mum says everyone is different," Zara said, after swallowing a big mouthful of cronzaki. "In fact, I was just thinking earlier how I could be more like you." Lottie jerked her head up to Zara, amazed. The amber lighting of the beacon of the wall softly illuminated the blue and gold-flecked skin on Zara's face. Lottie saw it was her new friend who now looked like she was faraway.

"I know my mum wishes sometimes I could be quieter," Zara admitted now, then cracked a grin. "Even now I can't sit still!" She added, she gesturing to her swinging legs. "When you say stuff, Lottie, it sounds really clever and thought-through." It was Zara now who wore a little frown, concentrating on what she was saying.

"I just say loads of things that're on my mind. I usually regret it later!" Zara grinned again, then sipped at her juice. "You seem really good at understanding stuff," Zara added. "Like how our world works. You really respect our culture, too."

"Really? You got all that?" Lottie asked, surprised. Zara glanced to her again, nodding. "I just wish I didn't feel so uncomfortable around people," she added, sighing again.

"Maybe that's something that can change with time," Zara answered her with a shrug. "Or maybe, even if it doesn't, maybe you can just work on your shyness not necessarily being a bad thing. I'm sure there's lots of other things you're good at, too," Zara encouraged. Lottie gave a small smile at her friend's kindness.

"Well…" Lottie paused as she thought. "My teachers do say I'm quite clever," she admitted, in a small voice. She didn't like bragging, but maybe it wasn't bragging if it was true. "I love reading, too," Lottie went on, her voice slightly stronger. "My favourites are detective stories, like Agatha Christie. She wrote crime novels on Earth," she added, at Zara's questioning eyebrow.

"She was born about a hundred years ago, Earth time, but she's so famous people still love her books today," Lottie added. "She wrote about detectives, like Miss Marple and Poirot," she continued eagerly, warming quickly to one of her favourite topics of conversation. In her mind's eye, she was thinking of the Old Swan Hotel, where Aunt Susan had taken her.

"The books follow the detectives as they try to solve a crime, like a murder or something. Often, there are clues that only they spot. I quite like riddles too," Lottie added, smiling at her friend.

"Wow, that's great!" Zara replied warmly. "I'm not that fond of reading," she admitted. "I mean, I like books, but I find I don't stay in them long enough to really enjoy them, you know? I get distracted quite a lot. Sometimes I find it hard to concentrate in school. I'm not really trying to be naughty," Zara emphasised. "I just find it hard to pay attention sometimes," she concluded. Lottie nodded. There were a few girls and boys like that in her class at school.

"I don't think I'd cope if I went to Earth," Zara said now, cracking another grin. "I think I'd be running around all over the place, not sure what to focus on first. I can't swim, either, so I'd probably drown if I had to go through that pool in the cave!"

"Hopefully not," Lottie replied, then both of them giggled. "You know, I always thought I'd be intimidated by confident girls, who find talking to people so easy," she added, glancing sideways to Zara again. "But maybe I wouldn't mind if she was as friendly as you."

The two girls smiled at each other then. Zara opened her mouth to say something else, but before she could speak, they heard someone shouting.

"Who's that?" Lottie questioned, as they heard the voice again. A man sounded like he was very cross, but they were still too far away to hear what was being said. Then Lottie heard a second voice, a woman, who was just as angry. "Sounds like they're having a right row," Lottie said.

"Yeah," Zara agreed, just as a woman came into view, lit by a beacon on a wall near her. "Oh, that's Uradna," Zara commented. Her eyes narrowed as she peered through the darkness. "That looks like Opin, too—it must have been him shouting. They're both ambassadors," Zara explained. "Uradna is from Edowoda, the western city," Zara added in a whisper, though the two were still at a fair distance and speaking so loudly, Lottie doubted they were aware of anybody else.

"Opin is from Tilajin, the southern city. They're meant to be friends, so I don't know what they're rowing about," she added with a shrug. The two girls watched as the two officials continued their row, dimly visible against the darkened hedges but still too far away to be in earshot.

The two ambassadors moved closer. From the beacon of the wall near them, Lottie could make out them gesturing wildly at one another. They began walking in the direction of Zara and Lottie, towards the door that led back to the banquet hall. Their voices grew louder as they neared, still totally unaware anyone was watching them. Then, was it her imagination? Lottie thought one of them mentioned the word 'locket', but they were talking so loudly and quickly, she couldn't be sure.

"Oh," said Opin, as the two of them came to a sudden stop, spotting Lottie and Zara by the wall. Opin frowned, opened his mouth. "Ah…" he closed it again and coughed. "Apologies, we didn't see you there. I…" Opin started to say something else, but then his sentence just faded away into the evening air. Beside him, Uradna looked even more incensed, with her mouth drawn into a thin, angry line. "Good evening," Opin added abruptly, before walking past Zara and Lottie.

"Good evening," Zara replied brightly. She sounded so cheerful, compared with their angry row, that Lottie bit her lip to stop a giggle escaping. Uradna's mouth only tightened a little further, before she was quick on her feet, following Opin.

As they walked through the big doors back inside, the pair began arguing again.

"Looked pretty intense, whatever it was," Lottie commented. Zara nodded, giving a little shrug again. "Did you hear them say anything about the lockets?" Lottie added.

"That's what it sounded like," Zara agreed. "They were rowing so loudly, though. I'm not sure." Lottie stared at the doors the pair had walked through, wondering what had made them have such a big argument, especially if they were normally friends.

Giving a little shrug herself, Lottie then bent her head to finally take her first bite of the cronzaki, almost forgotten in her hand until now. It tasted just as heavenly as the one she'd eaten this afternoon. Instantly, Lottie thought it was worth having a dry mouth afterwards.

As she munched the wonderful combination of pretzel, cake and custard, Lottie reflected on everything that her new friend had said just now. She still hated feeling shy and anxious, but maybe Zara was right. Maybe she could get used to other people more as she got older, or maybe she could try not to be so embarrassed or beat herself up about it.

"Here you girls are," Guira said suddenly, coming through the doors. "I wondered where you two had got to. It's way past your bedtime, Zara. Lottie, you must be exhausted," she added.

"I am, actually," Lottie admitted. Maybe her tiredness was partly why she'd gotten upset before. Even with her nap before the ceremony, Lottie had, in effect, stayed up all night.

"Come on, then," Guira said with a wink, reaching for Zara's hand. Zara hopped from the wall to take her mother's hand. The three of them walked back towards the palace.

"Have you enjoyed your birthday, Lottie?" Guira added. Lottie's eyebrows rose as she thought.

"Um, yeah." In all that had happened today in reaching Orovand, seeing the ceremony and the feast, she had almost forgotten it was her eleventh birthday. "It's been fantastic!" Lottie grinned.

"Coming here... it's one of the best birthdays I've ever had," Lottie declared, as one hand reached up to clasp her locket. Even with feeling anxious and upset, she was having a wonderful new adventure! Suddenly, as she walked with Zara and Guira back to her temporary bedroom, Lottie felt a little sad at the thought of leaving the realm of Orovand.

Once she had said goodnight to Zara and Guira, Lottie quickly changed into her pyjamas again, carefully folding Zara's beautiful dress over a chair in the corner of the room. She went to the bathroom and brushed her teeth. The Gold Dimension had toothpaste too, but it tasted of strawberries, rather than mint. Lottie turned to climb into bed, when she remembered she was still wearing her locket. Quickly, she reached up to undo it.

"Oh, come on," Lottie muttered, annoyed with herself when the chain slid through her fingers and came to land with a soft thud on the carpet, "I need to take more care than that."

Lottie bent to pick it up and examined the locket, relieved that there seemed to be no damage—but it was unlikely to get any scuff marks from landing on such a soft floor. Carefully, Lottie lay the locket back in its black box that had still been in her dressing gown pocket. She put it the box down on the bedside table and got into bed.

The last thing Lottie saw before she blew out the candle was her jewellery box, laying slightly at an angle. Then, in the darkness, Lottie smiled to herself as her eyes slid shut, thinking of this amazing adventure she was having. As she drifted off to sleep, Lottie very much hoped she would wake up in the Gold Dimension tomorrow, rather than in her Aunt Susan's creepy old barn in rural Yorkshire.

Part Two

Chapter Seven

The same smile that she had fallen asleep wearing graced her features as she woke the next morning. It was the soft, comfortable bed she'd woken up in, not shivering in a scratchy mattress. Already, Lottie knew she had woken up in Orovand, not in her Aunt Susan's house.

Lottie rolled onto her back, opening her eyes to the gold flecks and swirls in the ceiling above her. She rose her arms above her head and stretched her legs as far as she could under the duvet, utterly content. At some point, Lottie knew she would have to go back to Earth, but she was quite happy for her adventure to last another few days yet. As much as she'd enjoyed the ceremony and the feast, Lottie thought it might be nice to explore Oruvesi and get to know Zara and her other new friends, without a sea of people constantly clamouring to meet her.

With another stretch, Lottie rolled lazily over in her bed, the edge of the duvet brushing gently against her cheek. Rustling her head against the pillow, Lottie's gaze fell to her bedside table. Then Lottie frowned, sitting up in bed.

Her black jewellery box was there on the table, but in a different position. Last night it had been laying diagonally, with one end almost at the far corner of the bedside table. This morning, however, it was horizontal, completely straight in front of the unlit candle.

A slight hammering began in Lottie's chest, even as she told herself she could have moved it in her sleep. Lottie sat up in bed, the instinct that something was wrong only settling further. For, if her hand had knocked the box during the night, would it really be that straight? She bit her lip, reaching for the box. The catch gave its distinctive click as it opened.

"What?" Lottie gasped. Her locket was gone. The line of black felt inside the box lay entirely empty, as if nothing had ever been there. Lottie leapt out of bed, horrified. Hurriedly she collapsed to her knees, hands flailing about.

Even as she frantically checked the covers, beneath her pillow and under the bed, Lottie knew she had little chance of finding it. She was completely certain the locket had been in the black box the night before, because she'd been so annoyed about dropping it. Lottie could also remember clearly how the box had been lying at an angle, when now it was straight. This left one terrifying conclusion.

"Morning!" Lottie jumped out of her skin as Zara sang the word from outside her room, knocking on the door. Lottie said nothing, still in shock, staring at the empty back box. "Are you still asleep?" Zara called, knocking loudly.

"No." Lottie blinked, warily getting to her feet. "Come in," Lottie added. The words sounded strange as they left her mouth.

"Morning," Zara said again, as she walked into the spare bedroom. "I brought you some more clothes…" her voice trailed away, seeing Lottie's stricken face. "What's the matter?"

"I think…" Lottie paused as she felt the start of tears welling, but she blinked them stubbornly away. "My locket's gone," she tried again, her voice far stronger. "Someone's stolen it."

"What?" Zara nearly dropped her clothes for Lottie on the floor in her shock, but now tossed them onto the chair where her dress still hung from the night before. "How awful! Are you sure, Lottie?" Zara then asked, stepping forwards. "You could've just dropped it somewhere, or something." Lottie shook her head sadly.

"I know I put it in the box, I'm absolutely certain of it." Lottie gestured to where the box lay open. "That means someone..." Lottie put her hand over her mouth, sitting down on her bed as her voice faded away. "Someone was here," Lottie whispered, the dreadful realisation creeping over her. "Someone was in my room," she muttered, feeling a bit sick. "They went up close to my bed-"

"You're sure?" Zara repeated, full of disbelief. Lottie took it as a good sign that evidently, thievery was not a common occurrence in Orovand. After a moment she nervously put her hand on her neck, exactly the spot where her locket should be.

"Okay, listen," said Zara now, folding her arms as she snapped into an action again. "This is what we're going to do," her friend suggested, frowning. "I'm going to go get my mum, she's only downstairs. I'll only be a minute," Zara added as Lottie looked up, aghast.

"It'll be all right, Lottie. Nobody's going to try anything again now, there's loads of servants and people about." Zara's voice was strong and reassuring, bringing some small semblance of comfort to Lottie.

"My mum will know what to do," her friend said firmly. Lottie's gaze lowered as she nodded, biting her lip. On impulse, Zara stepped forwards and took Lottie's hands in her own. "It'll be fine, I promise. Look, why don't you get dressed while I'm gone? I'll be back by the time you're done. Besides, the key's in the door, so you can lock it behind me if you like," Zara assured.

"All right," Lottie managed, squeezing Zara's hands briefly before her friend let go. She tried to smile, but it came out wrong. "I'll see you in a minute," Lottie said, hoping her voice sounded stronger. Zara gave a small nod and shot her a quick smile before hurrying out of the room.

Lottie rushed to the door and turned the key in the lock as soon as Zara was gone. She wished she'd done so the previous night, but how was she to know someone would come into her room? With everybody being so friendly and with all the palace guards about, it had never even occurred to her that she might not be safe here.

Lottie paced the bedroom floor for a few seconds, her face creased in dismay. Who had stolen her locket? Why? Lottie bit her lip, shaking her head. To distract herself from being upset, Lottie turned to the clothes on the chair that Zara had brought her.

These clothes were much more like what Lottie was used to wearing on Earth. There were black cropped trousers that came halfway down her shins. Next was a white top that looked like to a t-shirt, only with zig-zag patterns cut into the sleeves and high neckline. Yet Lottie barely noticed them as she dressed, so distracted was she by the awful thing that had happened. Mechanically, Lottie ran the brush through her hair a few times before pulling it up into the usual ponytail. She had just sat down on her bed again to wait when there came a knock on the door.

"Lottie, may we come in?" It was Guira, sounding worried and urgent. Lottie went to the door to turn the key again.

"Lottie, are you all right?" Guira asked as she strode into the room, Zara right behind her mother. "Zara said you've had an awful shock." Guira's concerned, caring face nearly undid her, so Lottie only nodded again. "Are you certain your locket has been stolen?" she added anxiously.

"Absolutely," Lottie answered firmly. Quickly, she explained to them how she'd almost dropped the locket and how the black box had been at an angle, but this morning it had been perfectly straight. At this Guira shifted her gaze to the black box, lying empty on the bedside table.

"At first, I thought maybe I'd just moved it in my sleep," Lottie was saying, "but then when I opened it..." her voice faded away as she stood up from the bed. "I'm certain it was stolen," she repeated. Guira regarded her for a moment longer, then she nodded.

"I believe you, Lottie. I'm so sorry. I need to think..." Guira faltered, frowning. She put a hand to her head, sitting weakly in the chair by the desk. For the first time, Lottie realised Guira was upset about something else besides the stolen locket.

"What is it, Mum?" Guira only shook her head slightly. "Mum, what's the matter?" Zara prompted, worry palpable in her tone. Guira now reached for her daughter's hand, raising her head to look between the two girls.

"Sorry," Guira murmured. "I'm still in a bit of a shock myself. Sadly, Lottie's locket being stolen is not the only awful thing to have happened this morning." The two girls waited as Guira took a deep breath. "I hate to have to tell you this," Guira said now. "Lord Jakad is dead."

"What?" Zara almost shouted in shock. Lottie's eyes

widened, taking a step back in sheer surprise. The ruler of Orovand's southern city had looked so healthy and lively the previous night.

"Taranai, Jakad's maid, found him in bed when she went to wake him up, about an hour ago," Guira explained. "Not everyone knows yet, so you'd better keep it to yourselves." One hand was still pressed to her forehead.

"Do you think he was murdered?" The earnest question came from Lottie. Guira dropped her hand, both she and Zara glancing her way, before Guira nodded slowly.

"They think so, yes," Guira confirmed sadly. "Taranai said he was in the prime of his health. We have people trying to figure out how he died," she concluded heavily.

"Mum..." Zara began tentatively. "If Lord Jakad was murdered, then could Lottie's locket be part of it?" Guira looked to her daughter. "What if the two events are connected?"

"Let's not worry about that now," Guira soothed, whilst Lottie's gaze became ever-more fearful. If it had been a murderer or his accomplice that had broken in, what if she was in danger? "We have no evidence of that, Lottie," Guira reassured her.

"Come on," Guira added, standing. Lottie noticed how she immediately took her daughter's hand again. "We must tell the king about your locket," she said heavily.

The three of them headed downstairs, only taking a small detour on the way to the throne room. Lottie followed them into a dining room, much smaller than the banquet hall the night before.

"You should both try to eat something," Guira encouraged, as a servant came and placed a bowl of what looked like porridge before her. Beside it was a glass of the gold-tinted water, still tasting like strong mineral water with a touch of honey-like sweetness.

With all her worries about her locket going missing and the revelation that Lord Jakad was dead, the last thing Lottie felt like doing was eating. However, the routine of eating breakfast every morning had been instilled into her for as long as she could remember. Indeed, Lottie could almost hear her mother reminding her brightly how she would need her energy and that breakfast was, of course, 'the most important meal of the day'.

Almost to stop Julie Armitage's imaginary naggings, Lottie duly picked up her spoon and tucked into her porridge. It was heated through, but still cool enough for her to begin eating straight away. The grain (not quite like oats) somehow tasted crunchier. There was a hint of sweetness, although as far as Lottie could tell no sugar had been added to it. There was also an earthy, spiced taste to the porridge, but it was like the taste had come from the grains themselves.

The other thing the girl noticed was that the porridge was quite light, so it was quick to eat. Lottie took a drink of the golden water, realising for the first time that she had not woken up dehydrated, despite the mini cronzaki she had eaten the night before. Had that spiced apple juice helped get rid of the salty taste?

Then Lottie shook her head slightly, beginning to shovel the porridge into her mouth even faster, almost to the point of indigestion. As if it mattered how thirsty she was, on a morning like this!

A few minutes later, her breakfast was quickly forgotten as they left the small dining hall to see King Karalius. As she walked there, she realised everyone was probably finding out about Lord Jakad. The atmosphere was almost too quiet and as they walked through the entrance hall, Lottie spotted a few servants whispering in the corners, thinking themselves unseen. Lottie gave a little frown, wondering how and why the ruler of Tilajin had been murdered. Was it possible others were still in danger?

"Right then," Guira muttered, as they came to the throne room doors. Her tone was grim and determined. She motioned for Lottie and Zara to wait outside, just like the day before—but in an entirely different context. Just then, Lottie would have easily swapped her anxiety yesterday with how awful she felt now, with her locket stolen.

How trivial yesterday's worries seemed now, Lottie thought, as she stood there outside the palace doors. She couldn't get what Zara had said out of her mind, about her locket and the murder being connected. Could the thief be in league with the killer? Could they even be the same person?

"You can go in now," a servant said, snapping her out of her thoughts. He opened the big doors, slowly creaking to admit Lottie and Zara. They stepped into the throne room at once, bowing low, then slowly approaching the throne.

"Your Majesty," the two girls then chorused together, raising their heads to where King Karalius sat. Guira stood on one side at the bottom of the palace steps, with Preto stood on the other. Beside his father stood Prince Andri.

Lottie noticed straight away how different his mood was. Yesterday his eyes had crinkled as he smiled, but now his brows were knotted thickly in anger.

"Guira has told me what has happened, Lottie," he said, his voice heavy. The king moved his hand to stroke his beard as he thought. "She's told me you are absolutely certain your locket was stolen."

"I am, Your Majesty." Lottie bowed low again as she spoke. King Karalius nodded, saying nothing for the moment. Lottie wondered if she should add anything, but the king hadn't said anything else and Zara had said to only speak when she was spoken to.

"If I might speak, Your Majesty," Preto said suddenly, stepping forward. King Karalius glanced to him, waving his hand to give him permission.

"It is indeed an awful crime," he began in his low, rumbly voice. "Though the lockets will have become dormant again after the ceremony," he continued, "a single locket could cause great harm to Orovand, if its power could be harnessed." King Karalius nodded gravely.

"Not only that, Your Majesty," Preto said soberly, turning his gaze from King Karalius to Lottie. If the locket is not returned to her soon, then the human child may be trapped in the Gold Dimension indefinitely."

Lottie's mouth fell open. Trapped in Orovand? It was such a beautiful, heavenly place, but the girl did not want the paradise to become a prison. The thought of never being able to see her parents again was unbearable.

"Do not fret, Lottie," King Karalius said quietly, his tone suddenly kinder as he saw how distressed she was. "We have plenty of time to find your locket. It is indeed possible that the theft of your locket and the death of Lord Jakad are linked somehow," he added grimly. "We must hope that if we solve one mystery, then the other may come to light. In the meantime, you can be sure of our hospitality," he said now.

"Thank you, Your Majesty," Lottie managed to whisper.

Her thoughts were faraway, entirely distracted with the fear of being stuck in the Gold Dimension forever.

"That is all for now, Guira," King Karalius concluded, waving his hand again. Guira bowed low. The girls took the ten paces back, then turned around. As soon as Lottie was on the other side of the throne room door, she broke into a run.

"Lottie, wait!" Zara called after her, but Lottie did not slow down. She carried on running, heading around the palace towards the gardens. A man near a hedge looked up from his wheelbarrow, but Lottie just kept running, until she spotted the low stone wall where she and Zara had slipped away from the feast last night.

Here, Lottie came to a stop, staring at the gardens in front of her. She hadn't been able to see them last night in the dark, but now the sun shone brilliantly onto endless rows of neat hedges and flowerbeds. The flowers were baby blue, pink, orange and purple, yellow and so many more colours. They were so spectacularly vivid Lottie wasn't sure if any flowers existed like that back on Earth, even in the most exotic jungles. Every hedge and flowerbed was surrounded by neat patches of turquoise grass.

Earth. Home. Lottie looked up to the sky, another wave of sadness coming over her. Above her was deep blue, with clouds as wispy and fluffy as ever. Some of them were tinted gold—Lottie couldn't tell whether it was because of the sunlight, or because of the gold particles from the ceremony that had ascended to the sky. Perhaps it was both.

Even though the day was as wonderous as everything else in this place, it now seemed tainted. No matter how glorious the surroundings, Lottie knew she couldn't enjoy being here. She was trapped until she got her locket back. Taking a deep breath, she tried to figure out what on earth (or, what in the Gold Dimension, to be more specific) she was going to do.

"Lottie!" She turned now to see Zara skid to a halt beside her. "I…" Zara's voice faltered a little. Then her friend stepped forward, firmly taking Lottie's hand. "I'm so sorry, Lottie." Normally, Lottie wasn't very touchy-feely, but right now, she was grateful for Zara's compassion.

"Thanks," Lottie muttered, squeezing Zara's hand back. Then, a moment later, she let her hand drop back to her side as she stepped back, bowing her head. Zara looked at her, entirely confused. "Your Highness," Lottie greeted, as Prince Andri joined them.

"Oh," Zara said, her expression clearing as she looked at Andri. "You don't have to keep bowing to him, you know," she added to Lottie.

"Definitely not," Andri agreed, as a small glimmer of a smile crossed his face. "I'm sorry about your locket, Lottie," he said, his expression sober. "I do hope you'll get it back."

"Thanks, Your—" Lottie cut herself short, before she gave him his title again. "Andri," she finished instead. Andri nodded, a corner of his mouth slightly twitching into a smirk.

"I came to find you, because I thought you'd want to know…" the young prince hesitated his face serious while he looked around, checking they were truly alone.

"Lord Jakad's body has been initially examined," he said quietly turning back to them. "They believe Jakad was poisoned. They're not sure yet, but they believe it could be to do with his goblet. There was a bit of water still in there," he added.

"No, hang on," Zara objected quickly, her eyes widening. "Wait a minute, if it's in his goblet… then it couldn't be, could it?" Andri only gave a small shrug. Lottie glanced between them with her eyes wide, confused.

"Lord Jakad's maid, Taranai, probably gave him the drink of water before he went to bed," Andri explained. "So, if it is poison in his goblet, they'll think she is the most obvious suspect."

"Except I don't think she'd do this at all," Zara objected. "Why would she want to kill her own lord? Even if she did want to murder Lord Jakad, she'd hardly do it here, with so many people at the feast watching her," she added with a frown. "I think someone's trying to frame her. Hey, I've got an idea!" Zara added suddenly, looking to Lottie.

"Why don't we try to solve this murder?" she asked, a little of her usual excitement back in her tone. "You told me last night how much you like detective books," she pointed out. "You never know, if we found out who did it, it could lead to your getting your locket back!"

"I'm not sure," Lottie replied, quietly. "This isn't a story from one of my detective books, Zara, this is a real murder." Despite the warmth of the day, a chill crept up her spine at the thought. "A real person killed someone, then someone else stole my locket," Lottie muttered. "Or they could be the same person. They might even still be in the palace!" Lottie folded her arms. "We're only kids, it could be really dangerous."

"Lottie's right, it could be dangerous," Andri agreed. But "It would be better than sitting around, though. Remember what Preto said," he added. "Not only could it be really dangerous if whoever stole it figures out how to use the locket's power, Lottie could be stuck here unless we find it again. We can't afford to be waiting for the adults to do everything. They could take all day just to figure out what kind of poison it was," he pointed out.

"Exactly! We'll be careful," Zara persisted eagerly. "Besides, with Andri with us, people will have to listen!" Her grin faded slightly, seeing Lottie's dubious frown. "Don't you want to find out who did this, Lottie? Don't you want to get you locket back, so you can go home?"

"Of course I do," Lottie replied. "I just..." Lottie paused, hesitating. Andri had a point—it would be much better to try to do something to help solve the case of Lord Jakad's murder and her stolen locket, rather than risk just waiting for the adults. "All right," she agreed, "but we'll have to be extra careful."

"We will, I promise," Zara said earnestly. "The first thing to do is probably to talk to Taranai. She'll be down with the other servants."

"If she hasn't been arrested," Andri warned. The girls stopped in their tracks to look at him, eyes wide. "Like we said, she's the most obvious suspect," the prince pointed out. "If Taranai is innocent, which she probably is, then like you said, someone is trying to frame her." Andri folded his arms now as he thought. "We may be what stops her being put in prison for something she never did," he suggested darkly.

"Yeah," Lottie murmured. Zara was looking at Andri, stricken, as if she'd suddenly realised how high the stakes were for Taranai, or how dangerous this could be. Lottie bit her lip, then, feeling extremely uneasy. She told herself to be brave.

"Come on, then," Zara muttered, only a little fearfully. "Let's head to the servants' bit. We haven't got any time to lose." As the three of them headed towards the back of the palace, going around the gravel path to an area she hadn't seen before, Lottie glanced once more towards the palace gardens.

The Gold Dimension still felt tainted and despite the sunshine, Orovand was feeling less and less like paradise. With that sobering thought, Lottie followed her new friends a little quicker, hoping they could solve the murder and find her locket without being in danger.

Chapter Eight

"Look, there she is." Andri pointed as they turned another bend in the gravel path. Lottie looked to see a small door, looking far more ordinary than the huge, ornate-double doors at the front of the palace. Lottie wondered if it led to the servants' kitchens and their rooms.

A little way from that door, where Andri was pointing, was Taranai. She was sat alone, on a bench with her head bowed, near a barn. From the loose straw scattered outside and the musty smell already reaching her nostrils, Lottie guessed it was the palace stables.

Sure enough, as the trio crossed the cobbles, three unicorns came out of the large barn buildings. The beautiful creamy creatures with flecked gold on their hides made Lottie feel a little calmer. Any chance of feeling better, however, died as soon as she saw Taranai looking up. In the moment before the maid stood, Lottie saw how terrified she looked.

"Your Highness," Taranai bowed, as she jumped to her feet. The young woman was wringing her hands together, to try to stop them from shaking. "Does… His Majesty wish to speak to me?"

"No, my father does not wish to speak to you," Andri shook his head. "We do, though." Taranai only dipped her head a little in response. Lottie said nothing, trying not to stare at the maid. She looked as though she was about to be arrested and carted off to prison, like Andri had said.

"We want to help you," Andri said now. "We don't believe you did this," he added, as Zara strode forward to Taranai.

"It's okay," Zara murmured. "Here, sit down. You've had a shock." Lottie noticed Zara had exactly the same kind tones as Guira did. No wonder her daughter was full of such compassion. "Did you notice anything unusual last night?"

"Not really," Taranai replied, her hands coming to clasp together again. "Only that…" she swallowed, looking back up at them. "When I went to the kitchen to get the water for my lord, Dien was still up, in the kitchen. He got the water from the tap, then I took it straight up to my lord. So, if anyone tampered with the water it was him, not me. I told His Majesty this earlier," Taranai said.

"Dien is the head butler," Zara muttered to Lottie. Lottie nodded, pursing her lips together in thought. Could it really be the butler? She knew from the detective stories she'd read that 'the butler did it' was such a cliché, but that didn't mean it couldn't be true.

"I also noticed that when I went past Criada's room on my way to bed, the door was ajar," Taranai continued. Lottie wondered who Criada was, but she kept her mouth shut, not wanting to interrupt Taranai. "Since her door was open, I knocked to ask her when the servants' breakfast was. I'm here so rarely, I'm still not used to the routines at the palace," Taranai added in explanation. "There was no answer. When I knocked and looked in her room, I saw it was empty."

"How interesting," Zara remarked, folding her arms. "Criada is the head housekeeper," she murmured to Lottie.

"So, Criada could have been out of bed at the time of the murder, potentially without an alibi," Lottie said. "If Dien was still up, too, he could possibly be another suspect, if we don't know when he went to bed." Lottie thought then that they could probably say that about most of the palace guests, but it was best to think of who they knew were still up, first.

"Oh, wait!" Lottie said suddenly, looking to Zara. "Do you remember those two officials that were having that row last night?"

"Oh, yeah!" Zara jumped up from the balance bench as she remembered. "It was Opin and Uradna, envoys from Tilajin and Edowoda," Zara explained to Andri. "When we went outside the palace hall after the feast, we heard them rowing pretty loudly," she added. "When they saw us, though, they shut up straight away." Lottie nodded.

"I wasn't sure, but I thought I heard one of them say 'locket'," Lottie said, folding her arms as she thought. "At the time they could've been arguing about anything to do with the lockets, but—"

"One of them could have known something about your locket, Lottie, or both of them," Andri chimed in. "Maybe that's why they were fighting." Lottie gave a small frown, thinking that there were several pieces of the puzzle still to be solved. "Would anybody else be up late last night? Or have any reason to be wandering about the palace?" Andri pondered aloud.

"Oh, I know," Zara replied eagerly. "Karoc would have been organising the carriage drivers to take the last of the guests home, after the feast. Then there's Preto... he would have been up most of the night, guarding the lockets. He's dedicated his whole life to protect Orovand, though," Zara added. "So it wouldn't make any sense for him to murder Lord Jakad, or to steal one of the lockets."

"That carriage driver wasn't very friendly yesterday," Lottie remembered, frowning. "He soon tried to be nice, though, when he saw I was human. Anyway," she reminded herself, with a little shrug. "Not being very nice doesn't make you a suspect, necessarily."

"So far, then," Zara said, "we've got Criada the head maid, Dien the butler, Opin and Uradna who were rowing…" she was ticking them off on her fingers as she spoke. "Then Karoc the carriage driver and possibly Preto, though it's very unlikely. That's six leads to go on."

"So far," Andri agreed. "The truth is, lots of people would have been staying up at the feast, after we went to bed. So, it could be hundreds of people."

"We need to figure out a motive," Lottie pointed out. "If we can figure out why someone would want to murder Lord Jakad, that could narrow down the potential list of suspects."

"I knew you'd be good at this," Zara smiled widely. "Don't worry," she added comfortingly to Taranai. "We'll find out who did this." She stood from the bench again. "What's our next move?"

"I think Dien," Andri ventured. "He might know something about how the goblet got poison in it if he was the one to give Taranai the water. He might also know why Criada wasn't in bed when Taranai knocked on her door."

"Your Highness," Taranai spoke up. The three of them turned to look at her. "I appreciate what you're doing, sir, truly, but… this could be very dangerous. Hadn't you better leave this to the palace guards? I'd hate for you to be unsafe on my account."

"Someone broke into my room last night to steal my locket," Lottie pointed out with a little shrug. "I was in pretty real danger then—someone could've harmed me if they'd wanted to." As she spoke, Lottie felt adrenaline start to buzz that she might have had a narrow escape.

"Besides, the palace guard are all over the place," Andri added. "Nobody's going to hurt us in broad daylight with them around. We believe you didn't do this," the prince then emphasised, as he straightened and squared his shoulders. "We're going to find out who really murdered Lord Jakad." Suddenly, his voice was more authoritative, sounding almost as grand as his father.

"Thank you, Your Highness," Taranai stood up hastily to bow again, then the three of them made their way from the stables back to the rear palace door. Lottie glanced once more at the cobbled stable yard, but the unicorns had gone.

"What?" Zara said abruptly, as she and Lottie almost walked into Andri, who had come to a sudden stop. Andri didn't say anything, merely pointed to their feet. "Oh! We almost didn't notice that," Zara added, eyes wide again.

Looking down, Lottie saw the cobbles were splattered with muddy footprints, leading from the stable yard. They then stretched right across the path Andri, Zara and Lottie were currently walking through, cutting between two patches of vibrant turquoise grass.

"These footprints must've been made very recently," Zara commented now, as the three of them stared at the ground intently. "The servants would've cleaned up every bit of mess yesterday."

"I guess we didn't spot them before, because we were looking for Taranai," Lottie murmured, looking back the way they had come.

It looks like they came from the stable yard," Lottie

murmured, looking back in the way they had walked. "Then, they just disappear," she added, for the footprints vanished just before the servants' door.

"Stables are muddy places," Zara commented with a shrug. "Maybe it was just a stable hand last night, or Karoc, after he'd finished with the carriages."

"Yes, it could be nothing," Andri agreed, "but maybe let's keep thinking about it. For now," he added, straightening again. "let's talk to Dien." With that, the young prince strode forwards on the path again, heading to talk to the head butler. Lottie and Zara then hurried after him, being careful to avoid the prints in case they really did mean something.

Andri turned the large handle on the door to the servants' kitchen. As Lottie followed Andri and Zara, she was now so used to seeing gold everywhere, she hardly noticed the tiny flecks of gold speckled all over the wooden surface of the door.

"Your Highness," the servants chorused, dropping whatever they were doing to bow towards him. It was then Lottie realised why Andri had straightened himself to full height.

"Afternoon, everyone, apologies for the disturbance," Andri replied grandly. Zara had been right earlier, Lottie thought. Nobody would dare stop the Prince of Orovand. "We would like to talk to Dien," Andri said now, as the servants straightened again.

"Of course, Your Highness," a maid stepped forward, giving a little smile. Right away, Lottie noticed the kindness in her eyes. "I am Criada, the head maid." Lottie fought not to react—this smiling lady was one of the suspects! She was the one Taranai had seen was out of bed. Her features were small but delicate, with her blue skin a little paler than the other people she had met so far. Her toffee coloured hair was tied back with pins.

"Dien is in his parlour, Your Highness," Criada said now. "If you'd like to follow me, sir, I'd be happy to show you the way." She gave another small smile to Lottie and Zara as she spoke.

"Very good, Criada," Andri answered. The head maid gave another bow before gesturing out of the kitchen. The servants, too, gave another bow before busying themselves again with their tasks. Lottie thought they looked like they were making bread.

As they followed Criada, Lottie glanced down to the floor and hid a sigh, to see the kitchen tiles were positively gleaming. For if whoever had made those footprints was a suspect and had come inside, there would be no evidence suggesting where they might have gone next.

"Dien?" The four of them came to a stop, as Criada knocked on the door. "His Royal Highness Prince Andriana is here to see you," Criada announced formally. The door to the butler's parlour opened immediately, revealing a tall man who bowed low.

The butler's hair was almost black in parts, but streaked grey in others—and of course, it was all flecked with gold. Dien also sported a thin, wavy moustache. He was tall and almost gangly, with his skin more like Criada's pale blue than navy.

"Your Highness, what an honour," Dien greeted, bowing extraordinarily low. "I see you have brought with you Miss Zara and Miss Lottie, sir," he added, as the three of them came in. "You are most welcome. Please sit, if it pleases you," he invited, gesturing some seats opposite his desk. "How may I serve you, sir?" he enquired, as Lottie, Zara and Andri sat down.

"I'll get right to it, Dien. Please, sit also," he added. Dien promptly sat, as per his instructions. "We just spoke to Taranai. It seems that currently, she is the most obvious suspect for the murder of Lord Jakad. I understand you were the last person to see Taranai before retiring to bed?" Lottie gave a side-glance to her new friend. He really was going straight to the point.

"Ah, a terrible tragedy," Dien sighed sorrowfully. "I myself had the pleasure at serving him at dinner, he seemed a most pleasant fellow. Yes, sir, that is correct, to the best of my knowledge," he added, sitting up slightly straighter. "The hour was late when Taranai came in." He idly smoothed his moustache with the fingers of his right hand as he talked.

"I think Lord Jakad had been up longer than most of the other party guests, talking to the few nobles who remained," Dien continued. "When he did retire, he asked Taranai to take some water up to his room." The butler leant forwards now.

"As I told some of the palace guard earlier this morning, Taranai saw me take the water straight from the tap," he said. "I added nothing to it. She then took it, heading directly… I assume," he amended quickly, "for Lord Jakad's room. I'm sorry to say it, Your Highness," Dien concluded. "If poison was found in the water, however—"

"That would make Taranai the prime suspect," Andri cut in. The butler bent his head again. The prince folded his arms, then, sitting back in his chair. "Did any other servants witness you get the water from the tap?" He questioned, his voice smooth and even.

"No, sir," Dien answered, shaking his head. "As the hour

was late, most of the servants had already retired to bed. Your Highness," the butler added, "may I ask why you are taking an interest in this? Would it not be better to leave it to the palace guard?"

"Lottie's locket has also been stolen," Andri replied seriously. "We believe this might be connected to Lord Jakad's murder. We hope that by shedding more light on these awful events, her locket may be found. Otherwise, Lottie may not be able to get home," he finished a little darkly.

"Of course," Dien replied, nodding. "How awful for you, Miss Lottie," he added, glancing to her in sympathy. "I do hope the culprit is caught soon, so you may return home in peace and safety."

"Thank you," Lottie replied quietly. His concern for her seemed to be genuine. "May I ask, Dien," she said, "did you notice any muddy footprints on the kitchen floor?"

"I did notice them, first thing this morning, before Lord Jakad was discovered," Dien answered, nodding again. "No doubt you spotted them on the path, Your Highness," he said.

"I thought perhaps it was a stable hand, as they are often last in, after doing the final check of the unicorns," Dien added, a thoughtful expression on his face. "The only thing is, sire, that all the stable hands know to wipe their feet before coming in, it's one of the first things you are trained to do, you see. All the boots were thoroughly cleaned yesterday evening, sir, only an hour before the ceremony began," Dien said now.

"We wanted everything to be spotless, with so many noble guests and to prepare for the ceremony, sir," he explained at their questioning frowns. "The stable boots are all kept together, but I noticed a pair was missing first thing this morning. Of course, sir," the butler added, "I didn't think anything of it, till I heard about Lord Jakad."

"That's certainly interesting," the prince replied vaguely. Andri then scratched his head. "Have you noticed anything else out of the ordinary?"

"Not that I know of, sir," he shook his head. "After I gave Taranai the water, I did my final checks of the evening and went straight to bed." He paused. "Is that all, Your Highness? Only that some of the guests will still need tending to—"

"Of course, I understand you will have your normal duties," Andri interrupted again. "I wonder, however," Andri added as Dien stood, "whether you might fetch Criada for us and allow us to talk to her here. We have a few questions for her on this matter, also."

"Of course, Your Highness. If it pleases you to wait here, I will bring her immediately." He gave a final, long bow before leaving the three of them in his parlour.

"If Lord Jakad was poisoned and nobody else was in the kitchen when Dien gave Taranai the water," Zara began slowly, as soon as the door was shut behind him. "Then that means it's her word against his, doesn't it?"

"Yes," Andri agreed, nodding as he sat back in his chair. "Like Zara said before, it makes no sense for Taranai to kill her lord here, now, when Orovand is watching. Dien has served my family faithfully for many years," he added with a sigh, stretching his arms above his head. "If it was Dien who murdered Lord Jakad, then we need hard evidence," Andri concluded.

"Absolutely," Zara nodded, "Because nobody is going to believe Taranai, a visiting young maid, over the head butler."

The three of them then lapsed into a silence while they waited. Lottie assumed Criada would be out doing some task or other, somewhere in the palace. She tried to reflect on what she knew and immediately wished for a notebook, so she could write it all down. So far both Taranai and Dien seemed to suspect the other, because of the water Lord Jakad had drunk last night. Poison in the goblet seemed to be the obvious murder weapon, unless the palace guard confirmed otherwise.

Then the next potential piece of evidence was the muddy footprints. Was it possible this was a coincidence? She thought, like Dien, it was extremely unlikely that a stable hand would leave their muddy boots on before strolling through the palace kitchen.

Lottie speculated that if it had been a silly mistake, the stable hand would want to clean the mess up in case they got into trouble, rather than leave it for the head butler to see this morning. Besides, if they had trod in all that mud by accident, that wouldn't explain why there were a pair of boots missing. Why would you move a pair of muddy boots, Lottie wondered, unless you had something to hide?

Then, if the footprints weren't anything at all, Lottie wondered, what else did they have to go on? There was Karoc the carriage driver—he would have been one of the latest to bed because of taking the guests to their homes after the ceremony. Opin and Uradna had been up late rowing, which could make them suspects. Had they mentioned a locket? Lottie frowned as she tried to remember, but neither she nor Zara had been sure that's what they were talking about. Lottie gave a little sigh—there was so much to think about. A notebook really would be handy about now.

"Your Highness," Dien knocked on his own parlour door before opening it, Criada following him. "I shall be in the kitchen should you need anything, sir."

"Thank you, Dien," Andri said, back to his regal voice. "Do please sit down," he added to Criada, as the butler shut the door behind him.

"Yes, Your Highness, thank you." As she sat, Lottie noticed straight away that she looked as distressed as Taranai had done outside the stables. Did she know something, or was she just upset about what had happened? It was hard to tell. "I have already spoken to the palace guards this morning, sir," she said.

"I'm sure," Andri agreed. "We just want to clarify a few things ourselves." Lottie was really coming to admire Prince Andriana's skills. She thought he was making an excellent detective. "Can you tell me what your movements were the previous night?"

"Well, of course, we were busy getting ready for the feast, Your Highness," Criada began. "I was overseeing the food being prepared in the hall," Criada said. "We had a mix of both chefs in the palace and outside caterers."

"Very good," Andri replied. "How about after the feast?" His voice was casual, not letting on he knew Taranai had seen that Criada was not in her room. Obviously, he wanted to hear her version of events first.

"It took a while to clear everything up, sir," Criada answered. "We were most anxious for everything to be clean and tidy for the next morning. I think I was one of the last to bed... I think it was only Dien doing the final checks. Taranai was still awake, I believe," she added then with a frown. "Lord Jakad was one of the last to retire to his chamber, so I assume Taranai stayed up to attend to him," she concluded.

"Indeed," Andri replied vaguely. "So, then you went to bed before Dien and Taranai?" he suggested neutrally.

"Yes, sir, that's correct, I retired to my room, but then…" Criada frowned as her voice faded a little. "I fell asleep quite promptly, but I was not sleeping long before a noise woke me."

"A noise?" It was Zara who spoke then, as Criada hesitated again, staring into the middle distance with a frown, as if the head maid was trying to remember something.

"Some kind of banging," Criada elaborated now. "At first I thought it was Dien locking the back door," she said. "The sound continued, though, so I wondered if someone might be locked out. I went downstairs to investigate."

"So Dien ensures the back door is locked? That is one of his final duties?" Andri clarified. Criada gave a gesture that was somewhere between a nod and a short bow.

"Yes, sir, but by the time I got to the kitchen, the noise had stopped. I opened the door, but no one was there."

"I see," Andri remarked, as vague as ever. "Did you notice anything usual about the kitchens, Criada?" Lottie guessed he was thinking of the muddy footprints. Criada only shook her head.

"What happened next?" Zara asked eagerly, whilst Lottie stayed quiet, thinking. If Criada was telling the truth about not seeing any footprints, then they would have been made far too late for it to be any of the stable hands. Also, the door would have been already locked by Dien, so whoever had come in would have needed a key. Lastly, there was this strange banging Criada said she had heard which could be another piece of evidence.

"I was about to close the door again," Criada said now, "when I heard sounds of an argument. I looked out to see Sir Opin and Madam Uradna walk past a nearby lantern on the wall, near the stables. They seemed to be heading for the back of the palace. They were arguing very loudly about something, sir," Criada revealed. Lottie's eyes widened.

"We saw them rowing just before we went to bed," Zara said at once. "That would've been at least an hour earlier, if not two, before you saw them," she added to Criada. "We saw them go back into the feast, so they must've gone outside again. Could they really have been up for two hours rowing?" Zara wondered aloud.

"Did you hear what they were saying?" Lottie asked Criada. She hoped to find out whether the housekeeper had heard them mention her locket. To her dismay, Criada shook her head.

"I'm afraid not, Miss Lottie. Although they were shouting, they were talking so fast I couldn't hear what they were saying." Lottie nodded. She had thought the same thing last night.

"It is not in my nature to gossip, sir," Criada then pointed out to Andri. "So, I shut the door, locked it again and went to bed. I didn't leave my room until the next morning, when another servant knocked on my door to tell me Lord Jakad was dead," she concluded quietly.

"Very well," Andri reflected after a moment, when Criada said nothing further. He briefly stretched his arms over his head again, then glanced back to the head maid. "You are certain you locked the back door again?" he asked suddenly.

"Yes, Your Highness." Criada half-nodded, half-bowed again. "I remember the key swinging on the hook." Her eyes roved uncertainly over her three interviewers. "If you have no further questions, sir," she began. "Then perhaps—"

"You may resume your duties," the prince granted, cutting in the same way he had done with Dien. "If you have nothing else of interest to tell us."

"Thank you, Your Highness." Criada stood, then bowed formally. With her form still slightly bent, the head maid departed the parlour and closed the door gently behind her.

"Well!" Zara burst out with a sigh, as soon as the three of them were left alone again. "I hate to say it, but this just seems to be getting more and more complicated."

"It generally does," Lottie agreed wearily, thinking of the murder mysteries in her detective books. Indeed, Lottie was tempted to start losing hope of ever seeing her locket again. "We need to talk to Opin and Uradna," Lottie said next, trying to work out their next move. "If they went back outside to row again for ages, then maybe they saw the person who made the footprints, or maybe they saw something else," she suggested with a shrug.

"We also need to know what they were arguing about," Zara chimed in. "Lottie thought they might have been rowing about her locket. I thought they might have said that too," she added.

"Yeah, but I wasn't sure." Lottie frowned then as she thought. "If Criada really did see them rowing, then two hours is a long time to have a big argument," she pointed out, folding her arms. "Especially if they're supposed to be friends."

"That's what I was thinking, too," Andri agreed, then stood. "Let's go find them, then," he suggested. "They'll be staying at the east wing of the palace, in the rooms reserved for the officials and nobles staying for the ceremony." With that decision made, the three of them left the parlour. Lottie only hoped talking to Opin and Uradna brought them answers, rather than more questions.

Chapter Nine

Rather than going back outside, Zara now took the lead, as they went back through the big kitchens. Servants stopped to hastily bow, hiding their confusion well as Prince Andriana of Orovand strode through the servants' corridors.

"I don't think they were expecting that," Zara giggled, as they ascended the main staircase that lead to the rest of the palace. Despite dark circumstances of Lord Jakad's murder and her locket being stolen, Lottie's mouth twitched. She was more certain than ever that she had made the right decision to try to solve the case with Zara and Andri. Even if they didn't succeed and she was stuck here, it was much better doing something with her friends than doing nothing on her own.

"Hey," Lottie said, stopping to point as she glanced out of a crystal window. Two familiar figures were stood in the palace gardens. "Isn't that them?"

"Yeah!" Zara replied eagerly. "Good spot, Lottie!" The three of them hurried outside, rushing towards the next possible suspects. The two officials were now sat on the low wall, near to where Lottie and Zara had been the previous night. Lottie frowned, wondering why Opin and Uradna had returned there. Could they be coming back to something they had seen? Or was it just coincidence?

"Your Highness," Opin and Uradna greeted a little stiffly, standing as Andri, Zara and Lottie neared them. Though they had been respectful, they were far colder and more reserved than Dien and Criada had been. Lottie wasn't sure whether it was because they weren't servants (and therefore didn't have to be as polite), or whether they were both just in bad moods. Maybe it was both.

"What an awful tragedy has taken place," Uradna said now, shaking her head. "The disappearance of your locket, also... how terrible." She clucked her tongue in sympathy to Lottie. "I heard one of the palace servants talking about it, a little while ago," she added, at Lottie's frown. "You'll find news travels fast in Orovand," she said.

"Indeed," Andri replied grandly. "We were wondering what you and Sir Opin were arguing about last night," he added, using the same tactic of getting straight to the point again.

"We were discussing the politics between our cities, Your Highness," Uradna answered, rather defensively. From the tone behind her words, Uradna obviously didn't think what they were rowing about was any of Andri's business, even if he was the Prince of Orovand.

"Did you notice anything out of the ordinary last night, Madam Uradna?" Zara's words were quiet and polite, striving to be more neutral.

"No, not that I remember," Uradna answered shortly. If anything, she sounded even more annoyed talking to Zara than talking to Andri.

"How long did your argument last?" the prince enquired next. The two envoys glanced back at him, from where they had been looking at Zara with narrowed eyes.

"Only for a few minutes after we passed Miss Lottie and Miss Zara," Opin replied, still very reserved. "We did not wish to continue the debate once we got back to the banquet hall."

"Of course," said Lottie rather loudly, covering up for Zara's sudden gasp. "So, you didn't go back outside again?" Lottie added.

"Certainly not," Uradna replied, giving Zara a strange look as she gasped again. "Opin and I parted company once we got back to the hall," she said, whilst Lottie nudged Zara to be far more subtle. Privately Lottie was surprised too, her mind reeling. Either Opin and Uradna were lying about not going back outside to argue, or Criada was lying about seeing them rowing when she opened the kitchen door, hours after Lottie and Zara went to bed.

"You said you were arguing about the politics concerning your cities," Andri said, partly because Opin was also giving Zara a strange look because of her gasp. "Can you elaborate at all?" Opin glanced back to Prince Andri and though he bowed his head, he also narrowed his eyes.

"I'm sure you understand, Your Highness, that the matter is confidential," he replied tersely. "That is why we took a walk whist everyone else enjoyed the party. We did not wish to be disturbed." Lottie thought that would explain why Opin and Uradna had stopped so abruptly as soon as they saw her and Zara by the palace wall. On the other hand, though, they had hardly been subtle. If they wanted to have a confidential conversation, why would they be rowing, shouting at the top of their voices? Unless they were so angry, they didn't care about being secretive anymore.

"Very well," Andri replied. His tone was still neutral, but Lottie wondered if he was getting frustrated at not getting further answers. "Are you sure you did not see anything?" the prince pressed, folding his arms. "You were, of course, one of the last people to go to bed."

"We saw nobody, apart from the servants," Opin confirmed strongly. "I saw that girl Taranai in particular, going to bring Lord Jakad his goblet of water. Wasn't she the one who found him dead the next morning? They think the water was poisoned, as I understand, sir," he added to Andri. "So it seems she is probably the murderer."

"We also saw Karoc, the carriage driver, still up," Uradna said now. The light brown strands of her hair blew gently in the breeze, with its specks of gold flickering in the morning sunshine. "Obviously, he was about to transport more of the guests, but... he seemed to be loitering. I thought at the time he might have been up to something," she added sharply.

"We already reported all of this last night," Opin said shortly. "Including the exact nature of our... disagreement," he added, after hesitating. "We will of course answer any further questions the king may have of us. I bid you a good day, Your Highness," he concluded, before Andri could reply.

"A good day to you as well," the prince replied, a little stiffly. Lottie could tell King Karalius' heir was not used to being spoken to in such a manner. After the two officials had given a final short bow, they left the palace gardens, leaving the three youngsters once again alone.

"Either they are lying, or Criada is," Zara surmised, vocalising exactly what Lottie had thought. "Do you think they're hiding something, Andri?"

"Almost definitely." He folded his arms. "City officials are perfectly entitled to keep their own areas of jurisdiction confidential," he said, frowning. "It just depends whether you really heard them arguing about lockets." He glanced to Lottie and Zara. "Or, potentially, if they know something about Lord

Jakad."

"You'd think they'd want to be as co-operative as possible, given there was a murder last night," Lottie ventured quietly. "You said Opin was an ambassador of Tilajin, right?" she added. "Wouldn't he have been friends with Lord Jakad and want whoever did this to be caught?"

"Maybe he is doing everything," Zara said. "Maybe he just doesn't think he needs to answer to us if they have already talked to King Karalius. No offence, Andri."

"None taken." He stretched his arms over his head. "They mentioned seeing Karoc, so we definitely know he was one of the last up. Maybe he saw something," he suggested with a shrug.

With that, the three of them walked back to the entrance hall, cutting through it again to get to the steps and the square outside. Lottie squashed the familiar feeling of excitement, for talking to Karoc meant seeing the unicorns again. She told herself they were in the middle of serious murder and theft cases. Yet, she just knew seeing the magical, beautiful creatures again would lighten her heart.

"There you are," Guira said as they crossed the velvet red carpet of the entrance hall. Her arms were folded, clearly waiting for them. "Your Highness," she greeted, giving a short bow to Andri. Lottie thought Zara's mother seemed a little cooler than normal.

"Good morning, Lady Guira," Andri replied, nodding to her in return. "We were taking a walk about the palace," he said casually. Lottie fought not to bite her lip. While what Andri said was technically true, because they had been walking around the palace that morning, it was far from the whole story. Andri hadn't mentioned the fact that they had been trying to solve Lord Jakad's murder.

"I was just talking to Criada." Yes, Lottie decided, there was definitely a hint of rebuke in Guira's tone. "I hear you've been making quite a stir downstairs this morning, sir, visiting the kitchens and having interviews in the parlour." With the wry edge to her voice, Lottie couldn't tell if Guira was cross or impressed. Perhaps it was both.

"We were just trying to help, Mum," Zara spoke now. Guira glanced to her daughter. "We think Lord Jakad's murder has something to do with Lottie's locket. Unless we find out who did it and get her locket back, Lottie may be stuck here." Guira's face softened in sympathy.

"I am sorry this happened to you," Guira directed to Lottie. "However, as good as your intentions are, I'm not sure this is the safest thing for you to be pursuing, Your Highness," she pointed out.

"I appreciate your concern," the prince conceded as Guira turned back to him, with a polite nod of his head. "However, there's also the matter of Taranai. Without further investigation, Taranai stands as the most obvious suspect. Yet," he added decidedly, "I do not believe she did this. I think she's being framed."

"Your compassion is commendable, Your Highness," Guira answered him respectfully. Lottie realised this conversation had suddenly turned into a battleground of words, waged out of politeness. "However, I must advice you to stay out of this, sir. Leave it to the palace guard, I beg you," Guira emphasised. "I assure you, You Highness, that Taranai would not be convicted without evidence."

"That is very reassuring," Andri replied vaguely. Lottie blinked, glancing between them. Guira's mouth grew thinner, almost imperceptibly.

"Very well," Guira answered at last, rather coolly. Zara's mum had obviously noticed that the Prince of Orovand had not agreed to follow her advice and stay out of it. "Did you take a turn about the palace gardens yet? The day is fine," Guira suggested. Anything to stop them from doing more interviews with suspects and witnesses, Lottie thought.

"Actually, we thought we'd go out front and see Karoc, Mum," Zara said brightly. "We thought Lottie might like to see the unicorns again." Lottie hid her surprise at her friend's boldness, in telling her mother exactly what they were planning. Of course, Zara hadn't mentioned the fact they were planning to talk to Karoc about Lord Jakad's murder.

"That sounds like a fine idea." Guira smiled at her daughter. "I have some business to attend to in court, if you'll excuse me, Your Highness," she then directed to Andri, giving him a short bow.

"Of course." He gave her a nod back. They stayed where they were for a moment, watching Guira leave through yet another door in the far left-hand corner of the palace hall.

"Nice work." Andri gave a low whistle and grinned at Zara. Zara simply smiled back, shrugging.

"Come on," she said. The three of them made their way across the entrance hall, heading for the ornate, huge doors to the palace.

"This will cheer you up," muttered Zara, as they descended the palace steps, gleaming almost painfully bright in the morning sunshine. Despite the dark circumstances of the morning, Lottie smiled. They were going to see the unicorns again, one of her favourite things about Orovand.

The majestic creatures stood faithfully beside Karoc's

carriage, as beautiful as ever. The sunlight made the flecked gold of their coats and horns sparkle even further. The sight brought some comfort to Lottie. Indeed, in that moment, she knew that even if she was stuck in Orovand, she would never tire of seeing these wondrous beasts.

"Your Highness," Karoc greeted, pausing to bow as he stepped out of his carriages. Lottie couldn't help but walk slightly nearer to one of the unicorns, so close she could reach out a hand. The black unicorn bent its head to sniff her fingers, while the white one darted its head from side to side enthusiastically. Lottie liked to think they were both saying hello to her.

"Miss Zara, Miss Lottie," he added politely to them. Lottie noticed that Karoc had a cloth and what looked like cleaning fluid in his hands. She fought not to react, telling herself it could be perfectly ordinary for him to clean his carriage, particularly after having so many passengers the night before. Yet, Lottie couldn't shake the idea that to do cleaning the day after the murder—especially now, when Lord Jakad's murder was public knowledge—was suspicious. What if he was getting rid of evidence?

"How can I help you, sir?" Karoc asked now, wiping slightly grubby fingers on the cloth. "Would you like to take a ride around the city?"

"Not just now, thank you, Karoc," Andri answered. Lottie gave a little frown as she regarded the carriage driver. He seemed far more friendly than when she had met him yesterday. Was it purely because he was talking to the Prince of Orovand? Or was he trying to hide something?

Maybe, though, Lottie thought, he was genuinely this nice normally. After all, yesterday he had admitted to being a bit stressed with getting things ready for the ceremony, as well as being worried that he would crash into Lottie, after she had run out into the road to get closer to the unicorns.

"We were just wondering if you saw anything unusual last night," Andri said now, in all casualness. "As you would have been one of the last ones awake." The somewhat amicable smile faded on Karoc's face for a moment, then he frowned.

"I have already spoken to the palace guards, Your Highness," the carriage driver replied, clearly avoiding the prince's question. His voice had gone cold suddenly. Was it just because he thought they shouldn't be meddling, or was he trying to ward them off? She couldn't tell if Karoc was acting suspiciously or not.

"Of course, we just thought we could try to help them in the investigation, if at all possible." Andri's voice was as regal and as smooth as ever. "You may not know that on the night of the murder, Lottie's locket was stolen." At this, Karoc's eyes widened a little in surprise. "We believe the two events could be linked. Also, Lottie may be trapped in Orovand indefinitely, if the cases are not solved," he continued. Karoc inclined his head to the prince, then glanced to Lottie.

"I see, sir," he answered vaguely. "That is a shame about your locket," he added to Lottie then, though his face was still mostly unreadable. "Well, as I told the palace guards," he continued, one hand rising to run through his short hair. "I drove the last of the guests to their homes after the feast ended. I took a party far to the other side of the city," he said. "So I was probably last to return to the palace. After that, I went straight home," he concluded simply.

"Did you see anything out of the ordinary?" Andri repeated his question. Karoc tilted his head a little to the left as he thought.

"Well, I did hear some angry muttering," he reflected. "As the last guests I was waiting for hadn't come out yet, I walked around to the back of the palace to the kitchens. I saw Criada standing at the doorway," he said, frowning as he remembered. "Then I saw Opin and Uradna arguing." Lottie's eyes widened slightly, as this would corroborate what Criada said about seeing the officials arguing. It also meant Opin and Uradna were lying about not going back outside again.

"When was this?" Zara asked eagerly. "Also, did you hear anything they said? What they might've been rowing about?" she persisted. Karoc shook his head.

"No," he answered simply. "I could hear the angry voices, but I couldn't make out what they were saying. It was quite late then," he said, "as it was the last fare of the night."

"Do you know anything about Lottie's locket being stolen?" Andri asked now. Karoc shook his head a third time.

"I'm afraid I don't know anything about that, sir. Everyone knows the lockets are mysterious and powerful. Maybe you should talk to Preto about it, he might know more about why someone would take it."

"Yeah, we thought that earlier," Zara said suddenly, as if remembering the Guardian of the Lockets. Lottie had mostly forgotten about him, too, after talking to Dien, Criada, Opin and Uradna.

"We would like to inspect your carriages," Andri said now. Karoc glanced to him, surprised. "Seeing as you were taking the last of them to their homes, one of them could have dropped something... it could be evidence."

"Well, if you insist, Your Highness, then of course, you'd be most welcome." Karoc's voice had hardened and no longer sounded the most obliging, but it was still civil enough.

"I'm afraid I do," Andri answered formally. Once again, Lottie was grateful that Prince Andriana was helping them. She was sure she and Zara wouldn't have gotten very far without his clear authority. "Have you cleaned all of the carriages this morning?" Andri asked pointedly.

"This was my last, sir." Karoc's lip had twisted slightly into a sneer as he spoke. Lottie bit her lip at the feeling of her anxiety creeping up on her again, at the prospect of him becoming unpleasant. In the end, though, Karoc merely stepped aside. "Be my guest, Your Highness."

"I thank you for your co-operation," Andri nodded to him again. The three of them stepped inside the carriage, looking as plush and luxurious as ever. Karoc was still outside and they soon heard him whistling a low tune.

"Anyone else think he's suspicious?" Lottie murmured, after she glanced back out to see him attending to the unicorns.

"Totally," Zara whispered in agreement. "The way he was cleaning stuff the morning after Lord Jakad died doesn't look good. What if there was some evidence he wanted to get rid of?" She hissed, voicing Lottie's thoughts exactly. "What if this carriage was used to transport the poison?"

"Let's not jump to conclusions," Andri reminded her, as they looked around. "The palace guard may well have already inspected the carriages this morning," he pointed out reasonably. "They may have even given him the all-clear to clean."

"He didn't seem too happy at letting us have a look around, though did he?" Lottie said, folding her arms. "Although, maybe he just finds it annoying if the palace guards have already looked," she added, thinking aloud.

"I was thinking about what Karoc said he'd seen," Zara commented now. "Karoc said he saw Opin and Uradna arguing, so Criada must have been telling the truth about that."

"Karoc didn't hear any banging noises, though," Andri said, pulling back the red curtain, laced with gold, to check there was nothing behind the pretty carriage window. "So it looks like Criada might have been lying about why she went downstairs."

"Yeah, that's what I was thinking, too... hello," Lottie muttered to herself, "what's this

?" She stooped further, sticking her fingers in deeper in the gap behind the soft padded bench. A triangle of white had caught her eye and now she pulled out a small piece of paper, carefully folded.

"Ooh, what's that?" Zara whispered eagerly. Lottie shrugged as she gingerly opened the paper, smoothing the creases with her hand.

"It looks like a riddle," Lottie murmured, her eyes scanning the few words quickly. "It says..." the girl stopped in sudden alarm as they heard Karoc's footsteps. Whilst Zara put the cushions carefully back into place, Lottie folded the paper again, stuffing it into the left-hand pocket of her cropped trousers just as the carriage driver appeared.

"Did you find anything, Your Highness?" Karoc said, his gaze roving slowly over the three youngsters. "A dagger underneath one of the cushions, perhaps, sir?" He added, a little sarcastically.

"Of course not," Andri replied, straightening himself up to full height. "I'm sorry for wasting your time," he said, carefully avoiding admitting whether they had found anything else. "Thank you for your co-operation." Lottie noticed it was the prince being sarcastic now, as the three of them clambered back out of the carriage.

"I sincerely hope my carriages had nothing to do with it, sir," Karoc said. Though his tone had been short, the slight sneer on his face was gone—the carriage driver only looked thoughtful. "Between the other carriages, we drove over a hundred people back to their homes," he pointed out evenly. "So, if one were to find something, it could have been from any of those passengers," he concluded.

"That would be most unfortunate," Andri agreed, with another formal nod. Although she hoped her body language was still casual, inside Lottie was almost panicking. Was Karoc purely being hypothetical, or could he be implying he knew all about that piece of paper with the riddle on it?

"I might offer caution, sir," Karoc said, his eyes darkening a little. "It may not be the safest activity, to investigate murder and theft. If the murderer is still out there, then…" his voice had hardened a little. "I would hate to see any of you harmed, Your Highness."

"I appreciate your concern, Karoc," Andri replied grandly. "I thank you for your faithful service. Good day." With that he turned to walk up the steps, leaving Lottie and Zara to follow. Lottie did so calmly, fighting against all her instinct to break into a run. She pushed hard against the idea of whether Karoc's warning had been threatening, or whether he genuinely wanted them to be safe.

What Lottie did know was that out of all the suspects they'd talked to that morning, Karoc was the one she was the most apprehensive about. The question was whether the head carriage driver in Oruvesi was implicated in the crimes, or whether he was just unpleasant.

"That was a close one," Andri muttered, whistling low as they entered the palace hall again. "I thought he was onto us for sure." Lottie glanced back to the carriages but saw Karoc was busy cleaning the carriage again. She'd been so distracted about getting away, she hadn't even looked back at the unicorns. There they were, though, sniffing the air and pawing around, oblivious to the murder that had happened first thing this morning. Lottie bit her lip. If Karoc knew about the note they'd found, she could only hope they were far away by the time he realised they had taken it.

"Come on," Lottie muttered urgently. "We need somewhere to go a bit more..." she paused, her voice fading as a place guard walked past. Suddenly, Lottie wasn't sure if she could trust anyone here at all. "More private," she said, once the guard had gone. "How about your room, Zara?"

"Sure," her new friend replied. "Let's go." They began walking, as casually as they could, towards the grand staircase that led to her bedroom.

"Wait, look!" Zara commented, making the three of them stop again. "There's Preto," she pointed. "He's just left the throne room."

"He must have been speaking to my father," Andri observed, following Zara's gaze. He then turned slightly. "Karoc's going," he murmured. Lottie turned as well, to see Karoc walking away from the carriages, a bucket full of cleaning materials in his hand. "This could be our chance!" he suggested. With that, the three of them ran over to talk to the Guardian of the Lockets.

Chapter Ten

"Your Highness." Preto turned and bowed, his low voice uttering Andri's title. "I am sorry about your locket, Miss Lottie," he added, his voice filled with regret. "Nothing like it has ever happened before in Orovand. I fear it is my doing, that I did not foresee this happening."

"It's not your fault, Preto," Zara said quickly, then frowned. "What do you mean, you could have seen it coming?"

"Because protecting the lockets is my responsibility, Miss Zara," Preto answered. "It is a duty long passed down by my ancestors. It is my duty to watch over the lockets," he said with a sigh, until they transport back to Earth with the dawn." His gaze shifted from Zara back to Lottie.

"Unless, that is, a human has come to us as you did, Lottie," the Guardian of the Lockets continued. "When we have a visitor from Earth, the locket stays in the Gold Dimension until the human leaves, then it can transport the visitor back home. I'm sorry, Lottie," he said, bowing his head. "Perhaps I should have kept watch over your locket longer, until you wished to return home."

"There's no way you could've known what would happen, Preto," Lottie answered him at once. "Besides, you knew I wanted my locket back. There was nothing wrong in giving it back to me. It's whoever did this that's to blame, not you."

"I thank you for your kind words," Preto replied, bending his head to her again. "Know that I would do anything in my power to help you retrieve it."

"Thank you," Lottie replied. A small smile spread across her face at his kindness. Much to her surprise, given her shy nature, she suddenly had the impulse to hug him.

"Could I really be stuck here forever, like you said this morning?" Lottie asked next, trying to sound dignified as she quashed the silly urge. "What if I get the locket back, could I then go home?"

"It depends when your locket is recovered," Preto answered, his face serious. "Your locket still draws a little power whilst it is here in Orovand, but it will soon fade. You have until tomorrow night," he told her pointedly. "After that, you would be trapped in the Gold Dimension until the next ceremony, a year from now." Lottie gasped.

"We'll get you back home, we promise," Andri declared earnestly, as Zara put her arm comfortingly round Lottie. Once again, Lottie found she didn't mind her friend's embrace at all.

"Preto, there's something you said I was wondering about," Andri added. "What exactly did you mean earlier, when you talked about the locket's power being harnessed? Do you think that's why someone stole it, so they could try to use it?"

"That would be my suspicion, sir," Preto answered the prince. "The lockets are most powerful when they are together. As you saw with the ceremony, when united, they generate enough power to last the Gold Dimension a single year," he explained.

"Normally, when the ceremony finishes, the lockets return

145

to Earth and become dormant, ordinary jewellery again, until the time comes for the next ceremony. However, if a locket remains in Orovand because of a human visitor…" he gestured towards Lottie, "the power within that locket takes far more time to fade. If the energy source of that locket could be harnessed during that time," Preto said heavily, "then it could have the potential to do great harm in Orovand." He looked between the three of them, his features as sober as ever.

"As we know, the cities of Orovand have been in harmony for centuries, since its first citizens walked upon the Gold Dimension," the Guardian of the Lockets continued. "However, if one wished to break that alliance, then the power of the locket could be used to distinct advantage."

"War," Andri muttered, cottoning on quickly to Preto's meaning. "You're saying that someone could use the locket to wage war." The young prince's eyes were wide with alarm. "How is the power unleashed?" was Andri's next question.

"If only I knew, Your Highness," Preto answered, dipping his head again. "My duty is to guard them, sir—I've left their mysteries to our foremost scientists," he added. "However, my fear is that since someone has risked stealing Miss Lottie's locket, then perhaps they have already found out how to use its power." Preto sighed here, then glanced to Lottie.

"Do be aware," he said plainly, "that only if you find the locket and its energy remains intact, will you be able to return home. It would be possible, even if you had to wait until the next ceremony." Lottie nodded in dismay.

"You have a unique bond with your locket, Lottie," he added. "This is why you miss its presence here so keenly. The rare human visitors we've had over the centuries have travelled here with their own locket, passed down to them from previous owners. Not any other," he emphasised. "Therefore, if your locket remains lost, or the energy inside it is somehow stolen..." his voice faded away here but Lottie gasped. Preto's meaning was clear enough.

"You mean I could be trapped here forever, if I don't find my locket?" Lottie felt like all the breath had gone out of her body.

"I am sorry to be the bearer of bad news, but it is possible," Preto warned, his dark eyes full of sympathy. "All of us at Orovand will do our utmost to ensure this does not happen, Miss Lottie," Preto said earnestly. "You have both my word and my sword. If you'll excuse me, Your Highness, if there's nothing else," Preto added. "I must return to my other duties."

"Of course," Andri said, his voice sounding a little strange. Preto gave a final bow, then left the palace hall. Lottie, Andri and Zara were silent for a moment, taking in this revelation.

Lottie's gaze wandered absently over the vast room with the ornate crystal windows, trying to let it sink in what would happen if they didn't find her locket, or if the thief was able to use its power. She would be stuck here in Orovand forever. It would mean saying goodbye to her whole life on Earth, the only life she had ever known. She would never see her parents, Aunt Susan or her school again.

Lottie swallowed hard as she reached into her pocket, clutching the note they had found in Karoc's carriage tightly. Right now, this potential clue was her only lifeline.

"Come on," Andri muttered suddenly, breaking the spell of their silence and kicking them back into action. "We need to move, Karoc looks like he's coming back." Sure enough,

Lottie and Zara saw Karoc out of the window, walking back casually towards his carriage. Without another word and without any hesitation, the three of them broke into a run.

They did not stop until Zara closed the door behind them a few minutes later. At last, away from Karoc and anybody else they might not be able to trust, they could finally talk openly about what they knew so far.

"Almost all of them could be lying," Lottie sighed, standing in the middle of the room with her arms folded. Zara hopped to sit on her bed, then looked up to Lottie, patting the space beside her. Andri had opted for the chair near Zara's dressing table.

"Opin and Uradna were definitely lying about not going back outside to row more," Lottie continued, as she sat down next to Zara. "We know Karoc heard them, as well as Criada."

"They could be lying about what they were rowing about, too," Zara chimed in, nodding. Still unable to sit completely still, she began swinging her feet aimlessly as her legs dangled off the bed. "Karoc didn't mention hearing a banging noise," Zara added. "So Criada could be lying about that. Or maybe Karoc just didn't hear it for some reason," she concluded with a shrug.

"Then either Dien or Taranai have to be lying about the water," Andri said, nodding. "If it was poison in his water that killed him, then it had to be one of them that tampered with it, unless we're missing something."

"Oh, it's so complicated!" Zara gave a big sigh as she flopped back onto her bed, her legs still dangling off the edge as she stretched her arms above her.

"Then there's the clues we have so far," she said, sitting up again. "There's the muddy footprints and the missing boots.

It's far too late to be from a stable hand, if Criada was telling the truth about not spotting the footprints on the floor."

"If Criada is telling the truth, then whoever it was had to have a key to get in, because Criada remembers locking the door," Lottie said, frowning. "There was no sign of anybody breaking in," she pointed out. "The fact they hid their boots showed they had something to hide."

"Then there's the clue we just found in Karoc's carriage," Andri concluded, leaning forward in his chair. "Did you say it was a riddle, Lottie?"

"That would be brilliant!" Zara said excitedly. "Lottie said she's really good at riddles," she added to Andri.

"I said I liked them," Lottie corrected hastily. "I never said I was any good." If she was honest with herself, Lottie knew she was pretty good at solving clues and riddles, but she still hated bragging... even if it was true.

"You're just being modest," Zara smiled, nudging her new friend from Earth playfully with her shoulder. Lottie gave a small smile back as she retrieved the clue from her pocket. "What does it say?" Zara asked eagerly, looking over Lottie's shoulder.

"Give me a chance," Lottie said as she unfolded the paper again, a smirk tugging at the corner of her mouth. "So, the first bit says 'I have it, I've put it in a safe place. In case I don't meet you later, here's the place where it's kept'," she finished quoting. "Then there's this clue."

"That could be talking about your locket," Andri said, his eyes widening. "The clue part of the message could tell us where your locket is! Do you think they were talking to the murderer?" He asked, starting to sound as excited as Zara. "Maybe the murderer and the thief are working together," he

149

speculated.

"Maybe," Lottie answered thoughtfully. "That would be a good theory. Okay, this is the clue," she said, "Here we go." Lottie cleared her throat and began to read.

"Though I am free, I am flat and fatigued.
A form who is walked all over is above me.
Despite this, I am in the top of what's created."

"You what?" Zara asked loudly. Her response was so outspoken and confused, Lottie giggled. "I suppose it's meant to be hard to understand," Zara conceded, cracking a grin.

"Yep, it's definitely a riddle," Lottie confirmed. "I'll just read it out again," she added, then slowly read out the riddle one word at a time.

"The thing is," Lottie said when she had finished, "riddles can be done in lots of different ways. It usually relies on multiple meanings, like synonyms. You know, different words that have the same meaning," she added to Zara's confused frown. "Like cheerful and joyful both meaning happy."

"Oh, ok," Zara said, nodding. "I get it now. So, if we figure out what the synonyms might be, we might find out where your locket is." She paused, then, peering at the riddle. "Any thoughts, then?" Lottie giggled again.

"Give me a chance," she repeated, smirking. "It might not be synonyms. Sometimes riddle uses imagery and metaphor... okay," she said, stopping from talking to herself more. "Let's think about it. The riddle is the object, talking about themselves so we have to figure out where it's being kept from what it says."

"Flat could mean something to do with the floor," Andri

suggested, thinking. "Or the ground. So maybe we look down rather than up."

"Probably, yeah," Lottie said, nodding, examining the riddle once more. "It says it's free, yet flat and fatigued. It's underneath a form who is walked all over."

"So, there could be two figures being mentioned," Andri pointed out. "First, there's the object, then there's the thing that's walking all over it."

"Wait, though, doesn't the last bit mention being at the very top? Yeah, look," said Zara, pointing. "The top of what's created. Top of creation…" she murmured, "could that mean the Mavi Mountains, do you think? Those are the highest things in all of Orovand."

"Yeah, possibly. That's the bit I'm the most confused about," Lottie admitted, roving her eyes over the riddle a fourth time. "How can something be on the ground, or under things, yet be at the top of all of creation? It probably isn't all literal," she concluded.

"What does the bit about being free mean, do you think?" Andri asked. "Or fatigued?" He sighed, running his hands through his hair. "It doesn't make sense," he burst out at last.

"It doesn't make sense yet," Lottie pointed out, trying to encourage him. "We know it must mean something, because the wording is very precise. It's looking at the whole thing at once that's confusing. We have to take it step by step."

"Okay, then," Zara nodded, pointing to the first line. "It's free, yet flat and fatigued." She frowned. "Even that seems to contradict itself. You think you'd be happy if you were free," she said.

"Andri had a good point when he said flat could mean the ground," Lottie replied. "What's on the ground that's

151

fatigued?" She frowned. "What are other words that can mean fatigued?"

"Tired," Zara answered, "bored, exhausted, shattered..."
Lottie nodded for her to continue. "Weary, sleepy, um..."

"That's great," Lottie said, then smiled at her friend. "Maybe one of those will help us work out the next bit."

"Free," Andri murmured to himself. "Not tied down, liberated, loose... maybe it means happy, like you said, Zara," he added. "What do you think the 'walked all over bit' means?"

"You guys are good with synonyms," Lottie grinned, then frowned again, thinking about Andri's question. "My mum's used that phrase before," she murmured to herself, "about me, in school. She says the other kids in my class think they can walk all over me, because I'm quiet."

"We have that phrase too," Zara nodded. "So, if the form is walked all over... is there a second figure, like Andri said, that's bullying it? Or manipulating it somehow?"

"Maybe," Lottie said, sighing. "It's hard to know what's metaphorical, or what we should take literally. We might have even said part of the solution, when we were listing words. I feel like we're close," she added, narrowing her eyes at the riddle, "but maybe we've lost it again."

"You said it wasn't just synonyms," Andri reminded her, "maybe something else is the key. How else do you solve them?"

"Well, there's imagery and metaphor. We've already got a bit of metaphor here..." she peered at the words again. "Describing an object like a person is fairly common. It could be homophones, too," she said.

"That's something else I read, in a book I have about

riddles," she explained, glancing to Zara and Andri. "It's when you have two words that sound the same, but their meanings are totally different. Like 'see' meaning sight and 'sea' meaning the ocean," she added.

"So, what would that mean, if one of these words is a homophone type thing?" Zara asked. "What did we say earlier for fatigued? Tired, weary, bored, exhausted…"

"Bored!" Lottie burst out, so loudly it made both Zara and Andri jump. "Sorry, but Andri said something about the floor. If it's a homophone, that could mean board, like a floorboard," she explained excitedly.

"Brilliant!" Andri grinned. "That works with both flat and fatigued." Then he frowned. "Wait, that would mean it's a floorboard that's free," he said, pointing. "How can a floorboard be free?"

"Free," murmured Zara to herself. "What did you say before, Andri?" She frowned, trying to remember. "You said loose," she said suddenly. "You can have a loose floorboard."

"That's awesome, Zara," Lottie smiled at her friends. "You guys are really good at this. I know floorboard doesn't make sense with it being at the top of creation, but let's run with this theory for now,"

"The next bit is this other form," Andri said, frowning as he read the middle line of the riddle again. "So, it would be over the top of the floorboard… walked all over fits, too because we walk on floorboards all the time," he added.

"So… it's something on the top of the floorboard that we walk over," Zara suggested. "The carpet?" She scratched her head in thought.

"Maybe," Lottie murmured, half closing her eyes as she tried to think. "It could be a rug, or… I've got it!" She burst out, opening her eyes wide again. "The thing my mum told me," Lottie began to explain. "She said, 'don't let the others walk all over you like a doormat, just because you're quiet'. The answer is a mat, or a rug," she said.

"Wow, okay!" Zara almost shouted, clapping her hands. "That's brilliant, Lottie. We definitely seem to be getting somewhere."

"Yeah, hopefully!" Andri said now. "So far, then, we've got that Lottie's locket is under a loose floorboard under a mat, if our theory is right," he summarised.

"Our theory comes into a bit of trouble here," Zara pointed out, nodding to the last line of the riddle. "I can't say for sure, but I doubt there's many mats or loose floorboards in the Mavi Mountains." The other two giggled at her sarcastic tone. "You said it might not be literal, right?" she added to Lottie.

"Probably," Lottie agreed. "I think our theory is right so far, because it makes sense of the riddle and it's talking about a place," she reasoned. "Maybe the last line is telling us where the locket is?" she wondered aloud. "I think Zara's right that it doesn't mean the Mavi Mountains." Zara cracked another grin at this.

"In the top of what's created," Andri murmured to himself. "What do you think it could mean, Lottie, if it isn't literal? Maybe it's another synonym or homophone?"

"Probably," Lottie nodded, her eyes scanning the riddle once again. "Top could be high, or big, or head," she suggested.

"What about created?" Andri asked. "It could be made, built, developed—" the Prince of Orovand stopped suddenly. All the colour had drained from Lottie's face.

"What is it?" Zara's voice was concerned, as Lottie slumped back to sit on the bed, stricken. Lottie read through the riddle once more to confirm she was right, but she was already almost certain of the answer. "Are you okay?" Zara prompted, sounding even more anxious.

"I think I know what the answer to the last line is," Lottie murmured weakly. She glanced up in dismay to her new friends. "We were right about it being loose floorboard under a mat," she continued, her voice slightly stronger.

"The next bit is telling us where the floorboard is." Lottie stopped here, biting her lip. It had been almost fun, trying to solve the riddle. Now she knew the answer, however, it was if she'd suddenly remembered they were talking about murder. This was dangerous, she reminded herself, not a game at all.

"You've already said the answer, Andri," Lottie explained at last. "Top is a synonym, meaning head. The second clue, 'created', is also a synonym, but then that's pointing to a word that sounds like something else. I think…" she paused, almost afraid to say the answer out loud. Andri and Zara had said nothing, anxiously waiting for Lottie to reveal it.

"Another word for created is 'made', like you said, Andri," Lottie concluded heavily. "The word 'made' then sounds the same as 'maid', as in servant." Andri gasped. She knew he understood.

"The head maid," Andri repeated slowly. "It's talking about Criada," Andri said heavily, just as Zara's eyes went wide in recognition. Both of them sat down on the bed beside Lottie. "The answer fits, as much as I hate to admit it."

"It was Criada who stole your locket," Zara murmured in shock. "She's been working at the palace for years. She was probably lying about hearing that banging noise, wasn't she?" Lottie raised her eyes to the ceiling, nodding slowly. Lottie had been struck by how kind Criada had seemed, so sympathetic about Lottie's locket being stolen and being so eager to co-operate. Was that all an act?

"Unless it was someone else who wrote that note," Zara said slowly, thinking aloud. "Maybe they planted the locket under her floorboard. They could be trying to frame her," she suggested.

"It's possible," Lottie admitted, looking at the note again, this time observing the style of handwriting. "We need to go to her room, to see if we're right," Lottie suggested. "We also need to see if there's any writing in her room. We need to find out if it matches up to this note," she said.

"We should go to her room now, before Criada is finished for the morning. If Karoc is in on it and he knows we found the note, she might've moved it already," Andri pointed out.

"Yeah, you're probably right," Lottie sighed. "I wonder who the note was meant for," she said now. "Maybe if she's the thief, then it was meant for the murderer. Perhaps they got split up, so she sent the murderer a note, saying she'd hidden my locket?"

"Maybe," Zara commented, frowning. "Come on," she added suddenly, standing. "We've got to get to Criada's room. Sometimes the servants change before going to lunch." With that, the three of them hurried out of her bedroom, heading once more for the servants' stairs.

Chapter Eleven

The scenery of the palace blurred by as Lottie sped after Andri and Zara. Her heart was thudding fast, but it was also heavy with the knowledge that Criada, the housekeeper with the kind eyes she had met first thing this morning, was also probably the one who had crept into her room last night to steal her locket.

If that note really was Criada's, then she was also in league with the murderer, leaving them a note to say where she'd hidden it. It was possible Criada was being framed, but Lottie already knew this wouldn't make sense, unless she was missing something. Taranai was already the perfect suspect, so there was no reason for either the murderer or the thief to try to pin their crimes on someone else.

As they descended the servants' stairs, Lottie's cheeks deflated as she let out all the breath she'd been holding. She still thought trying to solve the case of Lord Jakad's murder and the theft of her locket was still better than doing nothing, but she was beginning to wonder whether Guira had been right to tell them not to get involved. This really was dangerous stuff.

"The servants live down this way, on the other side of the kitchen," Zara said. Lottie only nodded, hanging back a little. A little bubble began to form inside her, as her fists curled almost by themselves. The reality of being trapped in Orovand for a year, maybe even forever, hit her again. She blinked rapidly, swallowing hard as tears threatened to form. Suddenly Lottie realised that in everything that had happened, she really wanted a hug from her mum and dad.

"Here we are," whispered Zara at last. This pulled Lottie back to the present and she saw they had entered a long corridor, with lots of doors either side. "This is where the servants live," she murmured. "Criada's room should be along here." Lottie peered down the bare passage.

"Their names are on the doors," Andri muttered in a low voice, stepping up to a door to take a closer look. "Come on, let's find her room." The three of them crept along the corridor, eyes peeled to see which room belonged to the head maid.

"Here it is," Zara called in loud whisper, spotting it about halfway down the corridor. Lottie and Andri rushed to her, while Zara put her head against the door. "I can't hear anything," she hissed after a moment, then glanced to Lottie and Andri. "Shall we try it?"

"Go on," Andri agreed. "I think she's still upstairs, though probably not for long. You both go in," he suggested. "I'll keep a lookout and make some excuse if I'm caught. Besides, they won't tell me off," he added, giving them a quick grin.

"Okay," Zara murmured. Lottie stepped back, feeling nervous again. Zara turned her doorknob with a gentle klick, before the door creaked slowly open.

"Empty," Zara muttered. The air spilled out of Lottie's lungs in relief. "See you in a minute," Zara added to Andri, before dashing into Criada's room. Lottie quickly followed, closing the door softly behind them.

"Oh," Lottie sighed, taking in the bedroom. It looked ordinary enough—sparsely furnished with a bed, a wardrobe, a desk of drawers and a chair. However, there was a large brown mat in the middle of the floor.

"I know," Zara muttered regretfully, folding her arms. "I was kind of hoping we were wrong about the riddle, too." Lottie nodded. "I suppose we've come this far," Zara said. "Let's see if your locket is here, before Criada comes back," she suggested. Zara went to one of the mat's edges, to begin to roll it up.

"What are you doing?" Zara asked urgently, looking up to see Lottie walking over to Criada's desk. "Criada could be back any minute!"

"I know, sorry," Lottie muttered distractedly, turning back to quickly help Zara roll up the carpet. The two of them began feeling the floorboards.

"I think I've found the loose one," Lottie added, as one of the planks of wood began to rattle as she touched it.

"Is it there?" Zara asked eagerly, as Lottie touched a bundle of thick material. "Quickly!" Zara hissed, as they suddenly heard Andri's voice, loud and regal, on the other side of the door. Hastily Lottie opened the bag onto the floor.

"Muddy boots!" Lottie gasped, her eyes widening in recognition. "That means it was Criada all along, who made the footprints we saw outside." She peered around in the bag, then felt underneath the loose floorboard again. "The locket isn't here," Lottie sighed, disappointed.

"Are you sure? Everything else has been right," Zara whispered frantically. They could still hear Andri talking calmly outside, as though nothing at all was the matter, so Lottie took the chance to check again—but it was no use. Both the bag and the space under floorboard were now empty.

"At least we've solved the mystery of the muddy

footprints," Lottie murmured, putting the boots back into the bag and stowing them under the floorboard. "That doesn't make sense, though," she frowned. "The locket isn't here, so maybe Criada got spooked about something—but why wouldn't she move the boots as well, if she was worried about getting caught?"

"Yeah, that's a good—hurry, someone's out there!" Zara hissed, as the girls heard a female voice booming in the corridor.

"I do hope that isn't Criada," Lottie muttered, as they dropped the floorboard back into place. As they were about to roll the carpet back, the door swung open.

"Well, what do we have here?" Criada's snarling voice sent a shiver up Lottie's spine. Her tone sounded so nasty, it made Lottie wonder how she had ever seemed kind. "What do you think you're doing in my room?" Criada barked, glaring at the two girls, crouched over the rolled-up mat.

"We found your riddle," Zara challenged loudly, straightening and folding her arms. "We've seen the muddy boots under here. We know it was you who made those footprints and hid the boots all along. We just don't know why."

"I see," Criada answered icily. "How do you know I haven't ever seen any riddle, or that bag before in my life?" she said. "Anybody could have snuck in here without me knowing. Like you did," Criada ended with another snarl.

"Because of this," Lottie said, getting out of her pocket a piece of paper, with writing on that she'd found in Criada's desk. "Your handwriting matches the note we found in Karoc's carriage," she finished triumphantly.

"That's why you went to the desk first," Zara realised,

glancing to her. "Gosh, you're clever, Lottie." The corners of Lottie's mouth twitched up into the briefest of smiles at the compliment.

"Well, you didn't find anything, did you? Even the muddy boots don't prove anything," Criada snapped. "No matter what was written in that note."

"Except whoever you were writing to clearly wasn't after muddy boots," Lottie replied, somehow finding her own nerve. "You were writing to the murderer, weren't you? You weren't talking about your muddy boots, you were talking about my locket. Only something's made you worried, so you hid it somewhere else. Where is my locket?" she challenged, her voice rising with passion. "You had no right to come into my room and steal it!"

"I wouldn't talk to me like that, if I were you." Criada's voice abruptly went soft, but somehow that was even more dangerous. "Especially if you think I'm in league with a murderer." She breathed her final word, suddenly taking a step forward towards them. Her lips twisted forward into a menacing smile. Lottie's eyes widened in horror as Criada pulled out a dagger from under her apron, all silver except for a gold diamond just below the hilt.

"Did you do it?" Zara's stricken whisper came, the two girls stepping backwards until they were pressed against the wall. "Did you murder Lord Jakad?"

"Alas, no, that was not me. I've never killed anyone, yet," the head maid added, taking another step towards them, brandishing the dagger in their direction. "In fact, I'd hate to make you suffer the same fate as him." Was her voice sarcastic? It sounded so soft Lottie couldn't tell, but each word had pierced through her as if she'd shouted. Lottie swallowed, trying to think. Was Andri still outside the door? Could she risk calling out to him for help?

"This way!" they suddenly heard Andri call. "There may still be time!" Criada straightened with a grimace, stowing her dagger within her apron. She tilted her head to them, pausing to give the girls a final sneer before she ran from the room.

"There she is! After her!" The booming voice of one of the palace guards echoed around the corridor, strong and reassuring. Lottie's arms pressed against the wall as she began to shake, feeling quite faint suddenly. Could she and Zara have been killed?

"Oh, Lottie," muttered Zara in relief. Wordlessly, the girls joined hands before coming into a hug. Lottie embraced her friend back tightly, breathing heavily. What could have happened didn't bear thinking about.

"Zara!" Guira cried as she ran into the door, just as several more of the palace guard tore through the corridor behind her in pursuit of Criada. "Thank goodness you're all right, both of you!" Zara leapt across the room and dived into her mother's arms.

"Are you okay, Lottie?" Guira asked anxiously. She gently disengaged one hand from Zara to take Lottie's shoulder.

"Yeah." Lottie took a few deep breaths, trying to steady her frantic heart. Then she nodded. "I'm fine, I think," she added, as Andri ran into the room.

"Are you both okay?" Andri asked urgently, alarm plain on his face. The two girls nodded. "I saw Criada wasn't going to buy my story, so I ran to get help as soon as she came into the room. Did you find the locket?" the prince added quickly.

"It wasn't here," Zara replied heavily. "We did find

muddy boots in a bag, though. It was Criada who made the footprints," she revealed. "It was Criada, Mum," Zara added, glancing up to her mother. "She stole Lottie's locket."

"We found this in one of Karoc's carriages," Lottie said now, taking the small piece of paper out of her pocket. "It was a note Criada wrote to the murderer. She also left a riddle to where the locket was hidden," Lottie explained.

"By the time we figured out it was here, though, it was gone. Criada must have moved it," Lottie speculated. "Although, I don't know why she wouldn't move the boots too, if she was worried about getting caught." Guira frowned as she wordlessly took the proffered note from Lottie, her mouth drawing into that thin line as she read it.

"Maybe she only had time to move the locket last night, but then had the boots to dispose of, so put them here instead," Lottie suggested with a small shrug.

"Perhaps that's why she came to her room before the servants' lunch," Andri thought aloud. "Maybe she didn't have a chance to move them until now."

"Lottie figured out it was a riddle," Zara said now, taking a step back from her mother. "We all helped, but she figured it out really." A smile now appeared on Zara's face, as if already forgetting the mortal danger they had all been in.

"The riddle meant it was hidden under the loose floorboard, in Criada's room," Zara continued. "So we came straight here to see if we were right." Zara smiled further, but Lottie stayed silent. She'd noticed how quiet Guira had become. If anything, she was only looking sterner.

"Wasn't Lottie clever to figure it out?" Zara almost beamed. Andri was now also looking away. It seemed Guira's disappointment was obvious to everyone apart from Zara.

"Yes," Guira said quietly at last. Her voice was almost as soft as Criada's had been, but with none of the icy venom. "It was very clever, but…" Guira's voice hardened as she trailed off, looking up from the riddle to her daughter. "Didn't you listen to a single word I said earlier, about staying away from all of this?"

"I…" Zara's voice faltered now, stepping back as she looked down at the floor, her face creased up.

"Did I not warn all three of you that this wasn't a game?" Guira's angry stare passed over of them. "You could have all been seriously hurt just now," she said, her voice a little gentler. "Even you, Your Highness," she directed to Prince Andri.

"We had to try, Mum." Zara's voice was quiet but firm, only shaking very slightly with emotion. "Preto told us that Lottie could be stuck here until the next ceremony, if we don't get her locket back to her by tomorrow. She may even be stuck here forever if it remains lost."

"Zara's right," Andri answered. Guira looked to him sharply as he straightened, looking as regal as he had done when they had interviewed the witnesses and suspects earlier. "Without us, we never would have found the note," he pointed out. "We would never have discovered that Criada was the thief."

"That may well be so, Your Highness," Guira returned, still sounding fairly cross. "However, that doesn't make it right that you got yourselves involved in this. Lord Jakad was murdered last night. Murdered, do you understand what that means?" she emphasised, looking between them again. "The same thing could've happened to you, when Criada found you in here."

"They were just trying to help." Lottie's voice was quiet and uncertain. With all the turmoil of her lost locket, the danger she had just escaped and the thought she could be trapped in the Gold Dimension, Lottie was fighting off tears again.

"I know they meant well, Lottie, but the king and I were so worried about you," Guira replied, her features softening again.

"Preto told us that the power of Lottie's locket can be harnessed," Andri told Guira now. "It could do great damage to Orovand. I believe it was worth the risk," the prince declared passionately, squaring his shoulders, "to help Lottie and to protect Orovand."

"Is that so, son of mine?" came the deep, powerful voice of King Karalius. Andri pivoted round, as the four of them at once bowed to the king.

"Your Majesty," they all chorused, as the king stepped into Criada's bedroom, turning to survey Andri, Lottie and Zara in turn, before his eyes gaze settled onto Guira.

"The palace guard have informed me that Criada has, for the moment, evaded capture," the King of Orovand revealed heavily. "Her involvement in these affairs is most disappointing." Lottie stopped herself from saying she thought that was a massive understatement.

"I do believe we were doing the right thing, yes, Father," Andri nodded. King Karalius turned his sharp gaze to his son and heir. "Without our help, we would not have discovered Criada was involved," he pointed out again. "I was doing what I thought best for Orovand, Father," he said. King Karalius hardened his gaze, just like Guira had done.

"That, for the time being, is not your responsibility,

Andri," the king reminded him. "Though I admit your work is impressive," he added, a smile twitching at his lips, "it was not right for you to go against our wishes. You could have all been seriously injured, as Guira says. However, I am grateful for what you have discovered," he concluded.

"It was Lottie who figured it out, really, Father," Andri said eagerly. "Lottie says she really likes detective stories back on Earth. She's really good at solving riddles, too." King Karalius turned to look at Lottie, who had lowered her gaze to the floor at Andri's praise. She felt anxiety creeping up on her again, as she became the centre of attention briefly.

"Tell me what you know so far," he instructed. Lottie wasn't sure if was addressing her or all three of them, but as adrenaline continued to be replaced by anxiety, she glanced to Andri.

"We saw Taranai first, on a bench outside the stables," the prince began, tactfully picking up on Lottie's hint. Quickly, yet concisely, Andri told his father about meeting Taranai, seeing the moody footprints, then interviewing Criada and Dien. He then recounted their interviews with Opin, Uradna and Karoc, who had all been far less co-operative.

"So, then we found the riddle in Karoc's carriage, Your Majesty," Zara chimed in. "We—Lottie, really—solved the riddle, which led us to Criada's room. Underneath the loose floorboard, we found the muddy boots, but no sign of Lottie's locket."

"A shame," King Karalius said. "Criada must have suspected this was no longer a safe place for the locket and hid it somewhere else. Perhaps she even discovered the note went missing in Karoc's carriage. Guard!" he barked suddenly, making Lottie jump.

"If you could hand over that note," King Karalius directed to Lottie. "We'll need the boots, too," he added. Zara jumped forward to find the bag under the floorboard again, as Lottie handed over the riddle to the palace guard.

Take Karoc into custody at once," he ordered, as Zara passed the bag with the boots over to the palace guard. "He must be questioned immediately about the note. Also, bring Sir Opin and Madam Uradna to the throne room, he instructed. "If they were arguing further, as my son says, then I must have a further conversation about the nature of their disagreement."

"Right away, Your Majesty," the guard bowed. "You three, with me," Lottie heard the palace guard mutter, as they went to arrest Karoc.

"Karoc drove many of the citizens home in that carriage after the feast, Father," Andri said, repeating the thought he'd had earlier. "It could have been any one of them who dropped the note."

"No doubt that will be his defence, my son," the king replied with a nod. "This may be true, it may not... we shall see," He glanced between Lottie, Zara and Andri once more. "In any case, I must insist, that you three leave it to us to resolve this matter, he emphasised. He fixed his regal gaze upon Andri.

"This is not a game," he continued, echoing Guira's advice. "It is a dangerous business. Do you understand, Andri?" he added sharply. "That is a direct order from your father and king."

"I understand, Your Majesty," Andri answered him formally. Watching King Karalius, Lottie decided that he made a very good ruler over Orovand. He was kind, but also stern when he needed to be, even to his own son. Lottie knew she would hate to be on the wrong side of him.

"Your Majesty," the four of them bowed again, as King Karalius gave a final nod. He then left the room, his regal cloak swishing behind him, shimmering with red, purple and gold.

"Come on," Guira said after a moment, wrapping an arm around her daughter. "Let's leave this dreadful room. You must be ready for some lunch." As Guira headed back out to the corridor with Zara, Lottie wondered how anybody could be hungry. Perhaps, though, after all they had been through this morning, with their investigating and nearly being hurt by Criada, Guira wanted them to do something more normal.

"Thanks for your help back there," Lottie said now to Andri, lingering a moment in Criada's room. She'd heard the murmured voices of Guira and Zara talking to one another and wanted to give them both some privacy. Andri seemed to sense this too, because he was also loitering, standing a little awkwardly by the door.

"It's fine," he replied, then gave a little smile. "I'm just glad we got back before either of you got hurt." He stuck in his hands in his pockets now, glancing back at her. "You're a lot braver than you think, you know."

"I…" Lottie paused as she bit her lip, immediately self-conscious. "Thanks," she replied, knowing he was just trying to be kind. He, like Zara, was turning out to be a very good friend. A silence filled the room for a few moments, but Lottie found it comfortable rather than awkward.

"No problem. Shall we go find Zara?" Lottie nodded and the two of them headed back down the corridor and climbed the stairs to the rest of the palace. As they went back into the entrance hall, Lottie realised, with a little surprise, that Orovand no longer seemed tainted.

Even though Criada had escaped, she still didn't have her locket back and they still had no idea who the murderer was, Lottie felt somehow liberated. Maybe it was the simple fact they had done something. Whatever else happened, they were the ones who had solved the riddle. Lottie no longer felt helpless, so she could even enjoy once more the gold sparkling everywhere and the pure shimmering of the crystal windows.

Chapter Twelve

"There she is," Lottie said a couple of minutes later, as they spotted Zara sitting at the end of one of the tables in the smaller hall where they'd had breakfast that morning. "Do you think they'll find the murderer?" she asked Andri, as they walked over to join Zara.

"I think so," Andri nodded, giving her a quick smile to reassure her as they neared the table. Could he tell she was still worrying? Was he able to spot that the anxiety, that made her go quiet and withdraw, was never far away? She tried not to bite her lip.

"We've already solved one of the mysteries, after all," he continued, swinging his legs over the bench next to Zara.

"I believe the palace guard will find Criada," Andri told them sincerely, as Lottie took a seat on the bench opposite them. "Once they do, hopefully they'll get out of her where your locket is and who the murderer is. You okay, Zara?" Andri added suddenly, glancing to her. "Sorry your mum was hard on you."

"Yeah, I'm fine," Zara replied brightly, but the redness of her blue and gold eyes told Lottie a different story. "She wasn't, really," Zara said with a sigh. "She was just worried about us. I know Lord Jakad's murder was scary, but it's easy to just get caught up in trying to solve it."

"I know what you mean," Lottie nodded, as Andri and

Zara looked to her. "It's like my Agatha Christie books. It can become easy to just get involved in the puzzles."

"We all did," Andri agreed quietly. Just then the palace servants gave them plates laden with lunch. Lottie's interest piqued a little at the sight of two small, sweet bread rolls that had been at the feast the night before. Next to them were strips of dark meat that, when she tried it, tasted a little like roast beef. It was flavoured with something else, but Lottie couldn't put her finger on it.

"Even if it wasn't the most sensible decision…" Zara frowned, as the three of them began to eat. "It was still worth it to do something to help Lottie and Orovand like you said, Andri," she added, glancing at the prince. The prince nodded, his mouth full.

Bacon, Lottie realised, as she ate more of the meat. That was the other flavour—she was eating beef that somehow also tasted of bacon. With the sweet roll, it was like eating a burger. Next to the meat and the bread were long green beans, far bigger than any on Earth. They didn't seem to have any kind of dressing or sauce, yet they had a spicy kick to them.

"That's an interesting thought," Andri said now, gesturing his fork in Zara's direction. "Is it ever right to do something bad, to disobey rules in order to help someone and do good?" He swallowed a mouthful of beef, then set his fork down to tear his small roll into chunks. "Or, should you stick by the rules, always knowing you could have done something to make things better?"

"I don't know," Lottie replied, honestly. Zara carried on chatting with Andri about it, but Lottie drifted off from their ethical discussion. Her locket was never far away from her thoughts. She wondered now that Preto might have been right, about a bond between herself and her locket.

After all, when Lottie had found the bundle under the loose floorboard, even though she'd been saddened to know Criada was the thief, she had been filled with pure joy at the prospect of finding her locket again. Then, to find the muddy boots, but not her locket, had been bitterly disappointing.

Lottie could tell it wasn't just about getting back home, as much as she was missing her family. She was also desperate to get her locket back, to feel the gold chain securely around her neck. How could she have formed such a strong emotion about getting back something she hadn't even owned a single day?

"Oh, hello," Andri murmured suddenly. Lottie blinked, snapping back to the present. Her new friends had stopped discussing philosophy and were now looking behind her. "What's going on over there?" Lottie turned around in her seat, to see two palace guards and Guira talking to Taranai.

"It looks like good news, whatever it is," Zara commented a moment later. Taranai was clutching hold of Guira's hand, relief written plain on her face. The maid was smiling, but the slight quavering of her lip hinted she was still upset. No wonder, Lottie thought, given all that Taranai had been through that morning. After a few more moments, Taranai left the palace hall.

"Maybe Taranai is in the clear?" Zara suggested quietly. Guira was walking towards them, a wry smile on her features at knowing she'd been observed.

"Hey, Mum," Zara said. "What was all that about?" Guira pursed her lips, as if deciding whether to tell them.

"Well, I suppose there's no harm in telling you," she decided, coming to sit on the bench next to Lottie. "You might well try to get it out of Taranai herself, but I'd rather leave her to rest." Guira set her elbows on the table, leaning forward.

"The goblet of water Taranai gave Lord Jakad last night has been thoroughly examined," she began. "Thank you," she said, pausing whilst a servant walked past collecting empty cups. "Both the goblet and the water are free from any contaminations," Guira revealed.

"What?" Zara said loudly. Guira widened her eyes quietly, gesturing her hand to motion that her daughter should keep her voice down. "Sorry, Mum," Zara added in a deliberate whisper, also leaning forwards. "Was Lord Jakad even poisoned?"

"Yes, we're sure of that," Guira nodded firmly. "However, the water wasn't how the poison got in. They think it might have been something else he ate or drank."

"It might have been something from the feast," Andri suggested. "We all ate the feast food, though, didn't we? What is it?" he added suddenly, looking at the horror on Lottie's face.

"When we talked to Criada and asked what she was doing last night," Lottie murmured, her mouth dry. "She said she was in charge of catering, supervising the food."

"Oh, my goodness, you're right," Zara muttered, clapping a hand over her mouth. "Do you think Criada gave him the poison, then? Was she lying when she said she wasn't the murderer?"

"There has to be someone else involved, because of the note," Andri reminded her. "Unless she left the riddle on purpose, in Karoc's carriage," he said, eyes widening. "Maybe, in case she got caught as the thief, she wanted evidence to make it look like she wasn't the murderer as well.

Maybe she was even trying to point the blame on Karoc, in case she got caught."

"Does that make sense, though?" Lottie asked. "If you were the murderer and the thief, it seems really complicated to fake a riddle and leave it somewhere, just as your contingency plan. We could just easily have never even found that note," Lottie pointed out.

"Besides, we wouldn't have even known Criada was involved, if we hadn't found the note. So, she ended up incriminating herself as the thief," Zara shrugged.

"Yeah," Lottie nodded. "The evidence definitely points to someone else being involved. There must be something else we're missing," she frowned. "Some other way Lord Jakad got poisoned. It could have been one of the servants, or one of the guests who had the poison on them, Lottie shrugged. "In lots of ways, we're back to square one."

"I can see why the three of you wanted to get involved," Guira said wryly. "You're quite the detectives. That doesn't mean you should do any more investigating though. Are we clear?" she added, her voice suddenly sharp.

"Clear, Mum," Zara nodded. "It's like you said, Andri. Our best hope is in the palace guard getting something out of Criada, if they find her."

"They will, I'm sure," Guira tried to assure them. "The good news for now is that Taranai won't be framed for this. The palace guard are already interviewing the rest of the kitchen staff. Hopefully, someone will have noticed something. They also have a list of all the guests they're working through, but that will take time," she continued soberly.

"We don't have a lot of time, though, do we?" Lottie burst

out helplessly. "If we don't find my locket by tomorrow night, then I will have to wait until the ceremony next year to go home. Or, if we never find it, I'll be stuck here forever," she said bitterly. "That's without even thinking of what might happen to Orovand if someone somehow uses the energy in my locket. What if the lockets don't power your world properly next year?" Lottie lowered her gaze to the table, fighting tears.

"You can see why we were investigating, Mum," Zara said quietly. "We couldn't just sit back and do nothing, while Lottie felt so worried. She's right about the lockets, too... it could do harm to Orovand, even if whoever's got the locket doesn't figure out how to use it," Zara pointed out.

"I know," Guira admitted heavily. "I'm so sorry, Lottie..." she paused to touch Lottie's shoulder as she spoke. "I can't imagine how hard this must be for you. However, I still have faith in the palace guard," she told them firmly. "They won't stop until Criada is caught. Then we can find out what she knows about Lord Jakad's murder." Lottie only nodded. In all honesty, Guira's words, though they were kind, hadn't really made her feel much better.

"I'm going back to the king now," Guira said. "I'll see whether I can help shed light on these awful matters." She stood, keeping her fingertips lightly pressed on the surface of the table. "I'll let you know, Lottie, the moment there's any news about your locket. Stay safe," she added, the merest hint of a reprove entering her voice again.

"We will, Mum, we promise," Zara replied sincerely. With a final nod, Guira left them to their meal, her steps echoing across the floor. Lottie stayed looking at her plate, her fork still in her hand. Whatever appetite she'd had was fading quickly, but she made herself eat, partially so she had the excuse to not talk to Zara and Andri right now.

Lottie liked them a lot, but she knew they would try to reassure her that her locket could be found, that everything would be fine. She appreciated the sentiment, but she knew no matter how positive they were, she couldn't get her locket back through sheer will. They didn't even know whether Criada would be caught, let alone if her locket would ever be found.

"Why don't we go for a walk?" Zara suggested, after the servants came to clear their lunch plates away. "There's quite a bit of the palace gardens you haven't seen yet, Lottie. We could even go out into Oruvesi again, if you like."

"The palace gardens sound good," Lottie agreed. She didn't tell them she didn't want to leave the palace in case there was any news about Criada. Lottie couldn't explain it, but her instinct was telling her that the locket was somewhere close, maybe even in the palace.

"Sounds good," Andri echoed. As the three of them stood, Lottie caught a quick glance between Andri and Zara. Lottie hid a sigh, because this was how it always started. The other children in her class gave each other looks when she was quiet, subdued. Her classmates would feel awkward, not knowing what to say. Some of them would start to pick on her.

Lottie bit her lip, trailing behind Andri and Zara a little as they made their way back through to the entrance hall. She had enjoyed being friends with them, if only for a day. She'd hoped it would have lasted longer, but Lottie wouldn't be surprised if they now started avoiding her a little. They were too nice to tease her, but they might not want to be friends with her anymore, like some of her classmates who had once talked to her. Lottie sighed as she followed them out of the palace hall.

They emerged out into the afternoon sunshine, near where Zara and Lottie had gone outside after the feast the night before. Also, where only an hour or so ago, they had seen Opin and Uradna talking in low voices. As she walked behind them, she realised Andri and Zara had already struck up a conversation without her.

Andri and Zara chatted quietly while they walked between neat rows of hedges. To distract herself from feeling left out, Lottie looked around, taking in all the scenery. The lawns were as vivid a turquoise as ever. Flowers nestled tidily in their beds in brilliant hues of pinks, yellows, blues, purples and white. The petals were far bigger here, too, even on the smaller flowers.

The sun gloriously shone overheard, so that all about her glimmered. There was a peace about this garden, that soothed her uneasy soul. At least if she was stuck here, Lottie thought, she could take some comfort that she really would be trapped in paradise.

"I wanted to ask if you're okay." Zara's voice beside her made her jump. "Sorry," she said with a reproachful smile. "It seems a stupid question, to ask how you are. This must be so horrible for you." She glanced at Lottie, with her face creased in empathy.

"Thanks," was all Lottie said, her voice quiet, hiding her surprise that Zara had stopped her conversation with Andri to go and talk to her. "This is when the others at school stop talking to me, when I go quiet," Lottie at last admitted to Zara, swallowing the ball of emotion threatening to gather at her throat.

"That's horrible!" Zara repeated. "Just because you're quiet, doesn't mean others should ignore you." Lottie's mouth twitched a little. Perhaps Zara and Andri wouldn't avoid her after all.

"Thanks," Lottie said again. Andri had come to the other side of her now. Together, the three of them continued on the path through the palace garden. They had left the neat hedges behind and soon a small, clear golden pond came into view. The turquoise trees Lottie had seen in the distance were nearer, forming an avenue on either side of the path.

"Look," Andri muttered, pointing. "There's Karoc. They've obviously finished questioning him." They followed his gaze back towards the palace, where Lottie could now see the stables at a distance. Karoc was talking intently to one of the stable hands.

"Let's stay out of his way," Lottie suggested in a low voice. "Even if he has got nothing to do with it, we won't be his favourite people. King Karalius took him into custody because of us."

"I think you're right," Zara agreed, stretching her arms above her head. "There's Taranai," she said in surprise, lowering her arms again. Sure enough, Lottie glanced back along the path to see Taranai walking towards them. The maid had the same picture on her face as earlier—relieved, but still a little bit upset.

"I don't mean to be mean," Zara muttered as Taranai neared them, "but I'm a bit worried about talking to her, after what my mum said. What if we end up getting involved again?"

"We won't," Andri replied firmly. "She's only coming to talk to us, it would be rude to walk away. Good afternoon, Taranai," he said, as she stopped in front of them.

"Your Highness," Taranai came to a stop, inclining her

head as she bowed to him. "Miss Zara, Miss Lottie," she added, glancing at the two girls. "I wanted to thank all of you, for your faith in me. His Majesty the King has just declared me free of all charges, now we know the poison didn't come from the water in the goblet. I am very sad my lord is dead," Taranai murmured. "At least now I can grieve him fully, without fear that my king believes me to be the suspect."

"I'm so glad you're in the clear, Taranai," Zara said, smiling warmly. Taranai gave a small smile, then glanced to Lottie.

"I am grieved that this makes these terrible things even more complicated, Miss Lottie," Taranai said now. "As relieved as I am that the goblet found no traces of poison, I know that means it could have been anyone at that party who poisoned my lord."

"That isn't your fault, Taranai," Lottie replied, her voice still a little small, but thankful. "Who knows," Lottie shrugged, "maybe the palace guard will find Criada after all. Maybe she knows how Lord Jakad was poisoned."

"Perhaps, Miss Lottie," Taranai nodded. "I just wish I could help, or that he'd mentioned any kind of clue." The maid sighed, folding her arms. "I've been over it again and again in my mind, but he didn't really say anything, except…" Taranai shrugged, her voice trailing away.

"What?" Andri asked at once. Lottie shot him a quick glance, thinking of King Karalius' stern warning not to do any more investigating. She stayed quiet, however, because they were still only talking. Besides, there was some unknown instinct that told her Taranai could be about to say something pivotal, that could unlock the whole case.

"It was nothing of significance, really," Taranai

murmured, frowning deeper as she folded her arms again. "The only thing he did say was that he was particularly thirsty, as if he had salt in his mouth. He felt a bit dehydrated, so his last order to me was to make sure I refilled his goblet with fresh water. That's when I went to the kitchen to get the water from Dien," she concluded.

"Oh," Zara said. "Yeah, that probably isn't significant— what?" she added suddenly, at the expression on Lottie's face. The colour from Lottie's cheeks had drained and she looked as pale as when she'd solved the riddle. "What is it, Lottie?" Zara prompted, a little louder.

"I…" Lottie began hoarsely, then faltered. Lottie blinked, looking between Zara, Andri and Taranai. Could it really be a coincidence? Lottie thought. "I think…" she blinked again. "I think I've figured it out," she whispered. "We have to go to Oruvesi, to see if I'm right," she added, stricken.

"Who did it, Lottie?" Andri asked immediately. Lottie only shook her head, eyes wide. She couldn't speak about it until she was sure. Andri seemed to sense this, for then he nodded. "All right, let's go. We should tell Guira and my father about this, too."

***

"Mum!" Zara called urgently and a little breathlessly, as the four of them ran back into the palace hall, where Guira had been stood talking with the palace guard. She turned immediately to her daughter, distress already on her features at Zara's tone. Zara skidded to a halt in front of her mother. "Lottie thinks she knows who did it," she hissed.

"What?" Guira's alarmed gaze switched to Lottie,

standing next to Andri and Taranai. "After what I said at lunch," she said, her voice hardening slightly, "have you?"

"We weren't investigating," Lottie was quick to interrupt, desperate for her friends not to get into more trouble.

"That is true, my lady," Taranai confirmed with a nod of her head. "I was coming to thank Prince Andriana, Miss Lottie and Miss Zara for having faith in me, that it was not me who gave the poison to my lord."

"We then started talking about Lord Jakad," Zara said next. "Taranai was saying how Lord Jakad was thirsty which was why Taranai went to get him more water... I don't know," she shrugged, glancing to Lottie. "From that, Lottie seems to have figured it out."

"All right," Guira nodded, frowning. "So, you think you know who it was that murdered Lord Jakad, just from that?" Guira looked to Lottie too. "So, who was it?"

"I'm not sure, yet," Lottie managed to reply. "I mean, I hope I'm wrong... we need to check something first," she added anxiously. The more she thought about it, though, Lottie was sure she was right. "We need to go into Oruvesi," Lottie concluded firmly. At this, Guira's eyes widened slightly, drawing her mouth into a thin line. Lottie wondered if Zara's mother had figured it out, too.

"Very well," Guira nodded, looking grim. If she had worked out the identity of the murderer then she was also choosing to say nothing for the time being. "Come on, then," she muttered. With that, the five of them ran off in search of Oruvesi. As much as Lottie hoped she was wrong, part of her also hoped she was right—and that this could be the start of discovering Lord Jakad's murder.

Part Three

Chapter Thirteen

A few minutes later, the afternoon sun was gleaming upon the tall buildings as the five of them made their way through Oruvesi's streets, only slightly squished in the carriage. It wasn't Karoc who was driving them, but one of the other palace carriage drivers.

The weather should have had a serene effect upon them, but their mood was anything but calm. Lottie tried to keep her attention on the clopping of the unicorns, letting the reassuring rhythm of their hooves beating upon the gold-specked roads soothe her nerves a little.

Lottie kept her gaze out of the window, mainly so she could ignore the others glancing at her, especially Guira. Lottie was almost sure Zara's mum had figured it out, but so far, she had said nothing. Lottie wondered whether Guira, like herself, was just desperate to find out she was wrong. Next to her on the padded seat sat Taranai. She had requested to join them, saying that if they had found her lord's killer, she wished to look upon the murderer with her own eyes.

"What are we doing here?" Zara asked a few moments later, utterly bewildered, as the carriage came, at last, to a stop. They clambered out of the carriage, with Lottie still quiet. A breeze blew past, almost loud amid their silence. "What's going on?" Zara burst out a moment later, when Lottie still said nothing.

"Just wait, Zara." The instruction, slightly sharp, came from Guira. She was staring straight ahead of her, with the same grim tone. "Go ahead, Lottie," she said, nodding to her.

"Thanks," Lottie muttered, although she didn't really want to go any further. She wanted so much to be wrong. Yet there was something resonating in her, telling her to go forward. Lottie frowned. Could her locket be here, or was it just the powerful instinct that she was right?

Lottie took a deep breath, slowly letting out the air in her body again. She had to be like Poirot in Agatha Christie's books, to be brave and examine the evidence objectively. With that, Lottie straightened her head a little and began walking, towards what could be the biggest piece of evidence so far. She fought to keep her steps even, knowing it could lead to solving this case. Then, at last she came to a stop, staring around her.

It was the same square Lottie had entered shortly after arriving in the Gold Dimension. The busy centre of trade had once comforted Lottie with its normality, but now the deserted square was eerie and intimidating in its silence, not least because of what Lottie feared to find.

Her eyes drew back to the stall directly in front of her, looking as ordinary as it had done the previous evening. It was Dendari's market stall, where Guira had got her the heavenly cronzaki. Lottie stayed where she was for a moment, biting her lip, wishing the world could become still.

"Come on," Lottie at last whispered to herself. She crossed the final few steps to the stall, currently closed for trade, before walking around behind it. The stall was unlocked, which made Lottie nervous. Could Dendari be nearby, or on his way soon? All the more reason to be quick, Lottie thought, as she hunched down, beginning a hasty search.

There were different boxes of ingredients, underneath the covered tray of produce from the day before. Behind her was the large, long oven that took up almost entirely the back wall of the stall—but it was the ingredients that Lottie was most interested in.

A few minutes ticked by, as Lottie examined the boxes. Just as Lottie was about to hope she might have been wrong all along, she spotted it, sandwiched far down behind a box of flour. It was a small transparent bag, of course with the tell-tale gold hue. Lottie stared at the perfectly ordinary-looking bag of salt. She knew, entirely by instinct, that this was it.

Lottie carefully folded the flaps back on the boxes she'd moved and made everything tidy again, then picked up the bag of salt and hurried out of the shop. Why had Dendari left the shop unattended? Lottie wondered, as her gaze fell to her feet, moving quickly across the even, gold-flecked slabs. Had Dendari assumed they would never think to look in his stall? Or had he even planned for this eventuality?

"Did you find it?" Guira asked grimly, as Lottie neared her new friends again. She raised her head to meet Guira's expectant eyes.

"Yes." In her peripheral vision, she saw excitement enter Zara's face. No doubt they thought she was talking about her locket. "I think this is it," Lottie said, slowly holding out the bag to Guira.

"Salt?" Andri repeated loudly. He and Zara were looking utterly bewildered again. "What are you talking about?" he prompted in frustration. "What's salt got to do with any of this?"

"It was what you said, Zara, last night," Lottie spoke at last. Her voice was so quiet, the others had to strain their ears to hear her. "You said how Dendari originally came from the Mavi Mountains, that he was an expert on salt."

"Yeah..." Zara agreed cautiously, looking between the sombre faces of Lottie and her mother. Her own face was a picture of confusion. "I did say that, that's how he could bake the cronzakis to perfection. I don't see what that's got to do with any of this, though," she added.

"Taranai said that the last thing Lord Jakad said to her," Lottie continued, her gaze flicking to the maid, "was that he was very thirsty."

"Yes, Miss Lottie," Taranai confirmed, nodding. "He said he had the taste of salt in his mouth." Her eyes were wide. Lottie guessed that Taranai had now worked it out, too.

"We immediately jumped to thinking Criada could be the murderer, when we found out it wasn't in the goblet. Or one of the guests. What if..." Lottie swallowed. "What if it was an outside caterer? What if they were an expert in the salt that came from the Mavi Mountains, who made his signature dessert for the guests?"

"No..." Zara murmured, eyes flickering wide in recognition the way Taranai's had done. "You're saying Lord Jakad was poisoned with Dendari's salt?"

"You said he was an expert," Lottie repeated, nodding. "Out of all the people I've met so far in the Gold Dimension, if anyone could contaminate salt and make it lethal... then it's him," she concluded. "He was so nice, as well," Lottie sighed. "One of the first people to make me feel welcome here. I really wanted to be wrong," she concluded sadly.

"Could you be?" Guira then asked. Lottie glanced to Zara's mother to see a little hope had entered her eyes, but her face was still grim and resigned. "Dendari has been a friend of mine for years. He is so pleasant and mild-mannered, as you said." She shook her head. "I still can't believe he would be capable of this."

"The palace guards will soon determine a cause of death," Andri spoke now, folding his arms. "I suppose until then, this is conjecture. Though from what you've said, Lottie, it does sound likely. If salt is what he said he could taste before he died, then..." the prince shrugged.

"I wonder where Dendari is," Guira murmured presently. "If he was the one to murder Lord Jakad, then he could have easily escaped last night. He could be anywhere by now."

"Karoc!" Zara almost shouted. The others glanced to her. "If it was Dendari who poisoned Lord Jakad, then he would have been the one Criada wrote the riddle to," she quickly explained. "He would have dropped the note in Karoc's carriage."

"Brilliant, Zara." Despite having recently discovered that Dendari was in all likelihood Lord Jakad's cold-blooded killer, Lottie smiled. "Karoc might remember giving Dendari a ride. He might even remember where he took him! If he does, then we have a trail that leads to Dendari."

"Come on, then," Guira murmured. "There's not a moment to lose." With that, the five of them rushed back to the carriage. On the ride back to the palace, Lottie felt her anxiety growing at the prospect of talking to Karoc. This was secondary, however, to the urgency of trying to find out whether Karoc had given Dendari a ride. Karoc might even know where he was.

As they rushed into the palace, a couple of servants gave them a strange glance before hurrying away. Lottie could only imagine what a sight they were. The Prince of Orovand, one of the king's official advisors, her daughter, the human child and the servant of the murdered Lord Jakad, all rushing around as if their lives depended on it.

"Karoc!" Guira called, as they came to a halt outside the palace steps. Karoc was currently opening the door to his carriage so a lady could get out. Lottie vaguely recognised her as one of the court officials from the feast the night before.

"Lady Guira," Karoc greeted stiffly, walking around the carriage to meet them. "Your Highness," he added to Andri, his voice considerably colder as he gave a short bow of his head. "Are you here to inspect my carriage again, sir?" The sarcasm in his voice was clear.

"No, thank you," Andri answered formally. "We had to be sure you weren't involved, Karoc," the prince added pointedly. "The riddle was found in one of your carriages."

"Yes, the riddle," Karoc replied, folding his arms. "I never knew anything about that," he said curtly. "The palace guard only just let me go back to work. As I said to them, any one of the people I drove home could have dropped that note," he concluded defensively.

"Quite right, Karoc," Guira chimed in, before Andri could annoy the carriage driver even further. "We think the murderer…" She paused, obviously keeping quiet about Dendari for the time being. ""We think the murderer accidentally dropped a note in one of your carriages last night. It was written by the thief." Karoc gave a single nod at this, obviously unimpressed still.

"We do apologise for any inconvenience this may have caused you," Guira emphasised now. "We came to ask you," she added quickly, "do you remember whether you gave Dendari a lift in your carriage last night?"

"The baker, who made the cronzakis for dessert?" Karoc frowned. "Yes, I… I think I did," he confirmed, nodding. "Yeah, he was one of the last people I drove home. Looked shattered."

"I believe he was," Guira nodded vaguely, her voice sounding a little weak. The advisor then coughed, clearing her throat. "By any chance, do you remember where you took him?"

"Uh…" Karoc put his hands on his head, his elbows pointing outwards as he ruffled his hair. "Let me think about it." He half closed his eyes as he tried to remember. "I think it was quite far out, to the other edge of the city." Watching him, Lottie bit her lip, fighting impatience.

"He stopped at an inn at the city's edge, not far from Lake Purua," he added, his eyes opening again. "He said he had business in Tilajin the next day," Karoc concluded. "Why?" he asked then, with another frown.

"I see," was all Guira said, her voice grimmer than ever as she evaded his question. Lottie knew why, for Karoc's answer seemed only to confirm the theory that Dendari was the murderer. It was the typical cliché, that the guilty never ran.

"You may need to take us there, Karoc, for official palace business," Guira continued vaguely. "If you'll excuse me for a moment, I need to confirm something with the palace guard. Lottie, can I have that bag you found?" she asked quickly. Lottie nodded, handing it over. She guessed that the palace guard would be testing the salt to confirm it was the murder weapon.

"Stay here, Zara," Guira directed to her daughter, before heading into the palace. The rest of them remained near the carriage, just before the start of the golden steps.

"Does Lady Guira believe Dendari is involved in this awful business somehow?" Karoc asked, now sounding more curious than annoyed. Lottie said nothing.

"Dendari could have information regarding the investigation," Andri answered formally. Karoc merely nodded, though from his face he had clearly guessed there was more to it than that. As the silence between them grew, it began to get awkward. Lottie instead decided to look at the unicorns again, as serene and majestic as ever. Just gazing upon those beautiful beasts calmed her.

"Right," Guira murmured half to herself, as she emerged onto the palace steps a few minutes later. Lottie glanced to her. Although her blue and gold skin had not changed, Zara's mother somehow looked pale, as though she was about to faint. She took a deep breath. "Karoc," she said, "would you be so kind as to take us to the inn?"

"The carriage is yours, Lady Guira," Karoc responded with a regal gesture of his arm. "Your Highness," he added, his voice reserved but not quite as cold, as Andri followed Guira. All five of them squashed into Karoc's carriage this time. Andri and Guira were sat on one side and Taranai, Lottie and Zara on the other. Immediately, the carriage began tilting gently and the sound of the hooves' clopping upon the city streets filled the air once more.

"Why did you go into the palace, Guira?" Andri asked at once in a whisper, turning to face her. "What did you find out?"

"How Lord Jakad died, sir," Guira answered darkly, her voice as quiet as the prince's. "Or more specifically, how the poison entered his system." She sighed here, whilst the other four in the carriage waited with bated breath. "One of the palace guard chiefs has just informed me the autopsy of Lord Jakad is complete. They found poison on the traces of cronzaki that remained in his stomach," she concluded grimly.

"That means it was the salt!" Zara hissed, at this disturbing revelation. "It was Dendari who made the Mavi Mountain salt poisonous, for the cronzaki he must have given to Lord Jakad. Lottie, you were right!" Zara gasped.

"It looks that way," Guira said heavily. "The palace guard are checking the bag of salt Lottie found in Dendari's stall. It will most probably be a match to the poison on the cronzaki," she sighed.

Lottie said nothing, sitting back in the carriage. The evidence was growing against Dendari—he was an expert in the salt that came from the Mavi Mountains and she had just found a bag of probably poisonous salt in his stall. Then, of course, he had run away to the edge of the city. It would have been when Karoc took him to the inn, Lottie speculated, that he had dropped the note from Criada.

Yet, even in the face of all this evidence, all Lottie could think of now was Dendari's kind face, smiling as he welcomed her to Orovand. His easy demeanour had calmed her, as had the first cronzaki, that he'd given her free of charge. Would the heavenly snack be forever tainted now? Lottie bit her lip and frowned, mentally shaking away the image of him as the carriage drew them onwards. Now they were pretty much certain Dendari was the murderer, she told herself it was no good wishing he wasn't. Their best chance now was to hope the inn provided some clue to his whereabouts.

***

"I believe this is the inn, Your Highness, Lady Guira," Karoc called from the front of the carriage. He pulled the unicorns to a gentle stop. The journey to the south side of the city had taken a while, for the sun had begun to set. Oruvesi was far bigger than Lottie had imagined, when glimpsing the Gold Dimension's capital city just outside the cave. The sky was not as spectacular as last night, but the burning orb of orange dipping below the twilight horizon was still wonderful.

"We're almost at the edge of the city," Guira said, as the five of them got out of the carriage. "We just have to hope he isn't at Lake Purua yet."

"He probably lied, when he told Karoc he had business in Tilajin," Zara guessed. The others looked to her. "Maybe he wants to go to the Mavi Mountains, where he's from," she shrugged.

"Quite possibly," Andri nodded. "We have to hope he had a reason to stay in Oruvesi. Maybe it's to do with your locket, Lottie," he said suddenly. "We know Criada was writing the note to him, in case they got separated. Maybe he's still waiting for her here, so they can escape to the mountains together."

"Let's hope so," Guira muttered. "I'll go talk to the innkeeper, to see if he saw where Dendari went." As the others remained outside, Lottie glanced to the sky. Unlike the previous evening where daylight seemed like it would last forever, the sun seemed to be setting quickly. Lottie bit her lip, knowing that the next time the sun rose, it would either be her last day on Orovand or the first of many days stuck here without her locket. Possibly, it could be the first day of the rest of her life here, destined to be trapped in this beautiful place, far from home and without her locket.

"Don't give up hope, Lottie," Andri told her quietly. Lottie glanced to him to see his steady, determined gaze upon her. As their eyes met, he gave a small smile. "We've come so far. We know who stole the locket and now, almost definitely, who murdered Lord Jakad. We'll find your locket again, Lottie, I know it," he declared. Lottie's mouth twitched, wishing she could believe him.

"Right at the beginning, when we started investigating," Zara said from beside her. "you said it would be important to think of the motive. Maybe if we figure out why Dendari and Criada did this, it might help," she suggested.

"Yeah, I was thinking a bit about that on the way here," Lottie agreed. "Outside the feast, Zara, when we were talking about cronzakis…" Lottie's voice trailed as she frowned, trying to remember. "You said how lots of people used to live in the mountains, but not so much now."

"Yes, Miss Lottie," Taranai confirmed with a nod. "People liked living by the streams, leading from the mountains to the lake. My parents are originally from the Mavi Mountains," the maid explained. "The main town, near the base of the tallest mountain, was closed when I was small. Then my parents moved us to Oruvesi."

"Why did the town close down, Taranai?" Andri asked next. Taranai turned to him, inclining her head a little as the prince spoke.

"His Majesty King Karalius decreed that the mountain closest to the town was becoming unstable, Your Highness," Taranai replied. Lottie saw some sadness enter the maid's features. "The King believed rockslides could fall, making the town dangerous. I'm sure he spoke with justice and wisdom, sir," Taranai quickly directed to Andri. "However, in the twenty years since the closure of the town, no rocks have fallen. Some citizens—although not me, of course, Your Highness," she clarified. "They believe King Karalius closed the town on purpose, so people would have to move to the cities."

"Oruvesi has always been prosperous, as have the other cities, as far as I know," Andri pointed out with a frown. "I don't know why my father would make that order, if it wasn't true."

"I am sure His Majesty spoke what is right sir." Taranai bowed her head again. "I've heard tales from my parents that some people remain there, in small villages higher up. Without the main town for trade, those settlements are very poor," she said.

"That could be a motive," Lottie suggested. "Well, think about it from Dendari's perspective," she added, as the others glanced to her. "Say you had a business in that main town, but then suddenly your town is closed. Everybody's ordered to move away. You leave one of the cities, knowing you're leaving poor people behind who don't want to move, because their whole lives have been in the mountains. Dendari could have left family or friends," she continued, imagining the scene. "It could make him very angry with King Karalius, especially if no rockslides happened."

"That's certainly a motive for being angry with the king," Zara said, nodding. "Why kill Lord Jakad, the ruler of Tilajin, though? If you were cross about what King Karalius did, why not kill him directly? No offence," she suddenly added to Andri.

"None taken," the Prince of Orovand replied. "Well, my

196

father would've been far too closely guarded, not even a poisoned cronzaki would've gotten to him," Andri said thoughtfully.

"But wait, hang on," he muttered, his eyes widening a little, dropping his arms back to his sides. "Do you remember what Preto said earlier? He said that if someone could figure out how to use the power of Lottie's locket, then war could rage across the Gold Dimension."

"King Karalius said yesterday that the cities have been in a peaceful harmony for centuries," Lottie pointed out.

"Yeah, that's what my dad has always told me," Andri agreed. "He's also told me about how fragile peace is, though. Maybe that's why they needed your locket, too, Lottie," he said suddenly. "What if they used it, somehow, to make it look like the different cities were attacking each other?"

"That's it," Lottie breathed slowly, stricken, as Guira emerged from the inn to join them. "This has been about your father, Andri, but so much bigger than we thought," she whispered.

"The innkeeper said Dendari left first thing this morning, on foot." Guira sighed, speaking in a normal volume. "He turned right," she added, glancing down the street the way they had come. "So, at least we know he was heading back into the city, not towards the lake." Then she took in the horrified faces of Lottie, Andri, Taranai and her daughter. "What? What is it?"

"I think…" Andri coughed to clear his throat. "I think we've just figured out what Dendari and Criada's motives are." Still in hushed tones, the prince quickly recounted what they had worked out whilst Guira was in the inn.

"Oh, my goodness," Guira murmured heavily after he'd finished. Her eyes were stricken, the shock of it plan across her face. "They are trying to start a war, using the power of the locket?"

"That explains why they chose to murder Lord Jakad, too because he was the ruler of Tilajin. Think about this, too," Lottie said quickly. "Taranai is from the mountains. If she had been properly framed for his murder, then… she could look like a hero, if they did start a war, whilst Dendari and Criada escape."

"Taranai would always have been cleared, though," Andri pointed out now "The autopsy showed the poison was in the cronzaki, not in the water in Lord Jakad's goblet."

"You're right," Lottie agreed with some surprise. For a moment, she wondered what good all their investigating had done today—if Taranai would have been cleared anyway—but then they wouldn't have found the riddle in Karoc's carriage.

"We wouldn't have known about Criada being the thief," Lottie spoke aloud, folding her arms. "Taranai must have been framed to stall them somehow. Maybe Criada planned to make it look like someone from another region murdered Lord Jakad," she suggested with a shrug.

"Except we found the riddle and found the muddy boots," Zara said, so maybe that stopped whatever Criada was planning to do next. So, then Criada's option was running away, like Dendari did."

"Cowards," burst out Andri angrily. "We will stop them from waging war and get your locket back, Lottie," he emphasised.

"Let's think," Guira said, trying her best to keep her voice sound calm and normal. "If Dendari left this morning, going back into the city, what would be his next move? With both of our suspects gone, how are we going to find the locket?"

"We figure out how they planned to use it." The others turned to Lottie, at the sound of her quiet voice. "If we're talking about war across the whole of Orovand, then I doubt very much Dendari and Criada were working alone. We're going to need the king's help," Lottie said, glancing to Andri. "We need to find out what Opin and Uradna were arguing about."

Chapter Fourteen

"Do you really think Sir Opin and Madam Uradna were really in on it? That they knew what Dendari and Criada were planning?" Guira hissed, as Karoc sped them back towards the palace.

"It's possible," Lottie replied heavily, resting her head back against the padded cushion behind her. The day had been exhausting. Talking to Taranai after breakfast, then interviewing Dien and Criada in the butler's parlour, seemed a very long time ago. Next, they had talked to Opin and Uradna, before going out to meet Karoc and finding the note in his carriage. Finally, they had spoken to Preto briefly, before going up to Zara's room to solve the riddle, leading them to find the muddy boots in Criada's room.

Lottie shook her head slightly, for it didn't do her any good to think about what Criada could have done if Andri had not called for help. All of that only took them to lunchtime. Now, they had just discovered the evidence that pointed towards Dendari, the kind market baker, being the murderer. Lottie bit her lip, horrified at someone that seemed so nice could have committed such an atrocity.

Lottie sat a little more forward now, willing them to get back to Oruvesi faster. She could only hope that Opin and Uradna knew far more about Dendari and Criada than they were letting on, that maybe one of them knew about the plot to murder Lord Jakad. Perhaps, through them, she could finally get her locket back.

***

"Your Highness, Lady Guira, Miss Lottie, Miss Zara," Dien bowed, as the five of them quickly came through the vast palace doors a few minutes later. "Taranai," he added to his colleague, nodding his head to her.

"His Majesty has been waiting for your return, Your Highness, my lady. The palace guard have caught Criada," Dien revealed. "She is now in their custody."

"Brilliant!" Zara burst out, then lowered her head, far more subdued, at a single stern glance from her mother.

"It is indeed good news," Guira admitted then, a small smile forming on her face. "Hopefully, they can get out of her where your locket is, Lottie," she said. Lottie nodded, still reeling. "Come on, the king is waiting," Guira added.

All six of them went directly to the throne room, bowing low to King Karalius as they entered. Lottie guessed most of the palace staff were present, as well as most of the king's officials she had seen at the feast the night before. Lottie stayed where she was next to Guira and Zara, whilst Andri stepped boldly up the palace steps, inclining his head to his father before taking his place next to the throne. Dien and Taranai remained just inside the doors, standing next to the back wall of the throne room.

"Ah, my son," King Karalius reached to put his hand on Andri's shoulder. "All of you are most welcome," he said, turning to survey Lottie, Guira and Zara. His tone was still grim, but the fire of hope now sparked in his eyes.

"It is fortunate that Criada is back into my custody. She is currently being interrogated," he added sharply, anger and disappointment flashing keenly across his features. "She will then be left to reflect upon her treacherous deeds. I hope that by the morning, if not before, she will tell us where your locket is," he said to Lottie.

"I understand from Dien that you may know who orchestrated the murder of Lord Jakad," King Karalius said now, his gaze flickering to where Dien and Taranai still stood by the back wall.

"Yes, Your Majesty," replied Guira, bowing again. At this, he leant forward in anticipation. "It was Lottie who figured it out, before the autopsy even revealed how the poison got into his system," the king's advisor said, putting an arm around Lottie's shoulder. Lottie felt the king's eye move back to her, then he gave a single nod. Lottie swallowed, realising he was expecting her to relate all that had happened.

"Your Majesty," Lottie bowed, trying to sound a lot braver than she felt. She took a deep breath, then explained how all the evidence they had discovered pointed to Dendari.

"I must speak with Sir Opin and Madam Uradna at once," King Karalius declared now, standing from his throne. He gestured to one of the palace guard standing in the room, who immediately bowed and practically ran from the throne room to obey the king's order.

"I already spoke with them once, after Criada was discovered to be the thief," he said, placing clenched fists on the arms on the throne. "They assured me they were only discussing affairs of state." Then, King Karalius said nothing further. The rest of them stood silently, awaiting the arrival of the officials. Instinctively, Lottie knew this was it. This could be the final piece of the puzzle.

The throne room doors burst open a few minutes later. The palace guard stood aside, as Opin and Uradna approached King Karalius. They both bowed low to him, their expressions as unreadable as the king's. In the brief pause, Lottie understood, better than ever before, the idea of cutting the tension with a knife.

"Good of you to join us, Sir Opin, Madam Uradna," King Karalius greeted at last, his voice impassive. He stood from his chair, folding his arms again.

"You both assured me earlier that your argument last night was to do with the politics of your regions, utterly irrelevant to Lord Jakad's murder." His deep voice, though relatively quiet, still echoed around the throne room.

"However, we have since discovered the identity of Lord Jakad." King Karalius paused again, hardening his eyes into a glare. Everything was so quiet, Lottie could hear the king's heavy breathing through his nostrils. It almost made her squirm and she wasn't the one being interrogated by the king.

"We also found out that Criada and the murderer were working together," King Karalius revealed sharply. "They hoped to harness the power of Lottie's locket, to wage war across Orovand. I must ask you, therefore, whether either of you knew anything of these atrocious schemes."

"No, Your Majesty," Uradna gasped at once. "I assure you that I know nothing of such a plot. Lord Jakad was a close friend, Your Majesty," she continued. A single crack of grief permeated her words, "I could never have caused him any harm. However..." Uradna's voice faltered, her distraught gaze flickering to Opin.

"Sir Opin was speaking of the locket, Your Majesty,"

Uradna continued, stricken. Lottie's eyes widened. She knew one of them had been talking about her locket! Opin opened his mouth, but the king shot up his hand before the official from Tilajin could say a single word. The king nodded sharply at Uradna to continue.

Her voice still slightly shaky, Uradna continued, "On the night of the ceremony, we took a walk after the feast. Opin spoke of what a rare opportunity it was that the human child had come to Orovand. He was imagining what the locket could do whilst the locket remained in the Gold Dimension, if only its power could be harnessed."

"I was speaking only hypothetically, I assure you, Your Majesty," Opin returned quickly. King Karalius glared at the official speaking out of turn, but the king seemed to allow him to speak. "Madam Uradna thought I intended to use the locket, but I fiercely denied this," Opin emphasised. "Furthermore, Madam Uradna has no evidence whatsoever that I had anything to do with these awful crimes."

"I see." King Karalius spoke evenly, but with such ice in his voice it almost made Lottie flinch. "If you merely had a miscommunication, why did you lie to me, both of you?" he ended with a roar. "Why were you not honest, when I asked what your quarrel was about?"

"Forgive me, Your Majesty," Opin raised his head, remorse written plain across his face. "That was folly on my part. When I heard the news of Lord Jakad's death the next morning, I knew the quarrel would not make me look good. I convinced Uradna to say we were discussing politics."

"It was my folly, Your Majesty," Uradna added quickly. "Sir Opin persuaded me to keep my silence, because of how it looked—" at King Karalius' glare, Uradna fell quiet. Both of them had now broken the golden rule of speaking without being addressed. However, then the king graciously waved his hand to her, giving his permission that she could continue.

"Thank you, Your Majesty," the official from Edowoda bowed her head once more. "Opin convinced me that he had nothing to do with the theft of human girl's locket," Uradna said. "nor Lord Jakad's murder. I had not thought the death of my lord would be part of a greater scheme against your throne. I beg Your Majesty to forgive me," she added, her eyes pained.

"If the murder was to be the catalyst, that sparked war across Orovand, then it could not only be the work of my head maid and the baker alone," King Karalius said in summary, folding his arms. His eyes narrowed into a glare as he looked at Opin. Lottie was almost breathless just looking at the king, even though she was not the one receiving his penetrating gaze.

"Then, only an hour or two before Lord Jakad's murder, you are speaking about trying to take the locket's power. It seems you have incriminated yourself, Sir Opin," the king said darkly.

"Forgive me, Your Majesty," the official from Tilajin repeated. "That is precisely why I kept the details of our argument from you. I knew nothing of this dreadful scheme," he emphasised.

"Very well," the king growled, but his eyes were angrier than ever. He looked as though he might order Opin's execution on the spot, but the king was fair. He would not punish the official from Tilajin without further evidence. "That is all. Know we will be watching you closely, Sir Opin," King Karalius threatened.

"Yes, Your Majesty," Opin bowed low once more, before

making his exit. As Uradna bowed and began to depart too, Lottie caught the glare Uradna sent Opin's way. Lottie guessed the two would probably not remain friends.

King Karalius gave a curt wave of his head and the rest of them bowed low before departing the throne room. As they bowed low and began to walk out, Lottie wondered if Opin would head back to Tilajin as soon as he could, with the king as angry with him as he was, but then that would only make him look guiltier.

"You were right, Lottie," Andri stated, giving a low whistle, as they headed back down the corridor to the entrance hall. "I don't think I've ever seen my father so angry." He raised a hand to scratch his head. "Do you think Opin was really part of it?" he muttered.

"It's possible, sir," Guira muttered. "It's unlikely it's just a coincidence that Opin was talking about taking the locket's power the night before it was stolen, but he really might have had nothing to do with it. We'd need some hard evidence that connected him to Criada or Dendari," Guira said.

"We still don't know where Lottie's locket is either," Zara pointed out, glancing to her new friend. "That's still a big piece of the puzzle that we need to solve."

"I've been thinking about that, actually," Lottie replied. "Dien," she added abruptly, turning directly to the palace butler. "How did Criada get caught?"

"The palace guard caught her, Miss Lottie," Dien replied. "Only a few minutes ago, just as the sun went down." Lottie glanced out of the large crystal windows in surprise. She had been so engrossed watching King Karalius she'd not noticed it was already dark.

"The palace guard were doing an extra patrol when they

found her loitering just by the servants' back door," Dien continued. "It's such a shame," he sighed, "we worked together for over a decade. I never would have expected her to be capable of such a thing." He shook his head sadly. "If you'll excuse me, I must oversee the preparations for dinner. Taranai?" he added, looking to the maid, who inclined her head in his direction.

"Criada had escaped," Lottie said slowly, as Dien and Taranai headed back to the palace kitchens. She folded her arms as she turned back to Andri, Guira and Zara. "There's only one reason she would risk coming back to the palace."

"Your locket!" Zara agreed, nodding emphatically. "Criada must have stayed away after giving the guards the slip, waiting for it to get dark, before she risked going after it again."

"She was in a hurry to get it, too," Lottie said, trying to imagine Criada's motives. "Maybe where she hid it wasn't safe," she said, then frowned. Her instinct had been gnawing at her all day that her locket was close by somewhere. "Why would she be by the servants' door?" she murmured, frowning, then gasped, as the solution suddenly presented itself.

"Of course!" Lottie shouted, excitement and adrenaline quickly taking over. "Why didn't I think of it before! It's so obvious when you put two and two together!" Lottie smacked a hand against her forehead.

"Careful, Lottie," Guira admonished gently, yet smiling broadly at the thought Lottie might know where her locket was. "Take a deep breath, calm down and tell us."

"Yes, sorry…" Lottie managed, too distracted by her discovery. She felt like she and Zara had swapped places, because while she was almost jumping up and down, Zara was stood very quiet and still. Zara's eyes were wide, watching Lottie intently, waiting for the last mystery to be revealed.

"Right." Lottie took a deep breath, then smiled properly for what felt like the first time in ages. "What's the piece of evidence we've all forgotten about?" She was so happy and relieved she almost giggled at their blank faces.

"The footprints on the path!" she revealed triumphantly. The three of them frowned, clearly not with her. "When we first saw those footprints, we thought it was a stable hand just being messy, right? Then when Dien told us about the missing boots, we knew someone had broken in."

"Yeah, we thought it someone breaking in," Andri nodded. "Criada said she heard a banging. We found the muddy boots in her room, though," he said, frowning deeper.

"Exactly!" Lottie nearly shouted, then took another breath as she saw their confused faces. "Don't you see?" she added, almost impatient. "It's been staring in our faces this whole time! It was Criada making the footprints, so we know it wasn't anyone breaking in," she explained.

"Yes, she had the key," Zara agreed, frowning, folding her arms. "So, is the question why she would be faking intruding into the palace? Staging breaking in, for some reason?"

"No," Lottie answered, feeling like she was about to jump up and down again when she saw her friends still hadn't grasped it. "She wasn't pretending to break in, why would she be?" Lottie emphasised. "She wasn't breaking in; she was sneaking back in from somewhere. Somewhere those muddy footprints came from," she finished.

"Of course!" Andri almost shouted too, his eyes popping wide with the same excitement as Lottie. "You're absolutely right, Lottie, why didn't we see it?" He put his hands to his head. "Criada went into the stables to hide the locket, then must have gotten her boots muddy before coming back. She must have just made all of that stuff up about hearing a noise, because she realised, we'd noticed the muddy footprints. She was trying to throw us off."

"Gosh, Lottie, you're clever!" Zara admired for the second time that day. Lottie giggled at the compliment. "She must have panicked when she saw the boots, because all the others had just been cleaned that night, like Dien said."

"So, she took them to the one place she knew at that time—she hid them where she'd originally hidden the locket," Lottie said, following the logic. "She must have gotten paranoid for some reason, so she moved it from under the loose floorboards in her room. Criada must have been trying to get around the palace to the stables when she got caught," Lottie speculated.

"Yes, well done, Lottie!" Guira marvelled. "Come on, we haven't got a moment to lose," she added. With that, the four of them ran quickly to the stables.

***

"Don't mind us," Lottie grinned, almost giggling in joy as she bounded past a bewildered Karoc. For the first time since entering the Gold Dimension, she practically ignored the unicorns; such was her haste to find her locket. Lottie felt that same resonating in her soul, growing ever stronger. She knew she was right—her locket was here.

"Everyone, start looking!" she called out excitedly. The footprints had been cleaned from the inside of the stables, so they didn't have much to go on, but even that didn't dampen her high spirits.

"Lottie's locket is in these stables, somewhere," Guira explained happily to Karoc. "Don't worry, we know it isn't you," she said quickly, seeing the shock and dismay on the carriage driver's face. "Criada hid it here last night... never mind how, we'll explain later," she added, noticing the confusion enter his features. "Keep looking, everyone!"

Karoc joined in the search, as the five of them looked in every cubicle, every box and crate, every corner, nook and cranny. Tense minutes ticked by.

"Lottie." A whisper came from Zara, so quiet she barely heard it, but she did. Lottie jerked towards her friend to see she had found a roll of cloth in the palm of her hand. "I found it in a pot," she said in the same quiet voice. "Here," she added, holding it out.

"Thanks," Lottie whispered. There was a slight, delicate jangling, as the makeshift cloth parcel was placed into Lottie's hands. The resonating in the girl's soul grew far louder, like it was ready to burst. Unable to wait a moment longer, Lottie unfolded the cloth.

Lottie's locket lay safe and whole in her hand. Lottie clasped her fingers around it, letting the simple cloth fall to the floor, as she held the pendant and chain securely.

"At last," Lottie whispered. She felt wetness pricking behind her eyes, as tears of happiness began to fall. "I've got it," she murmured, moving to clutch it tightly to her chest, as if nothing in the world could ever separate her from her locket again.

Chapter Fifteen

King Karalius looked around his throne room with icy eyes and a locked jaw the next morning. In fact, Lottie wouldn't have been surprised if the king had heaved his ornate royal chair from where it was nailed to the carpet, only to throw it through one of the crystal windows.

She could well understand why, for the king was waiting for the guards to summon Criada before him. It would be the first time the king saw his former head maid since she had been captured last night, after so many years of her trusted service. The palace guards had kept Criada in the dungeons till this morning. He had hoped an uncomfortable evening in chains, would render her more willing to confess to her crime.

Lottie waited, stood anxiously with Guira, Zara and Taranai. Despite her abandoned joy at finding her locket, she had hardly eaten her dinner (something vaguely resembling chicken and rice). Lottie had gone to bed wearing her locket, then struggled to fall asleep. She was far too nervous about Dendari being missing.

Guira had suggested she could have gone back to Earth the previous night, but Lottie sensed the locket still had enough power—Preto had told her she needed to go home by this evening. Besides, Lottie needed to know her locket had not been tampered with before she used it to travel back to Earth. For what if he had something else to implement? What if he could still use her locket?

The palace doors burst open. Lottie and the others jerked their heads, as several guards trooped into the room. Three palace guards led the small procession, rhythmically tapping their tall spears to the floor as they marched. At the top of each spear was a gold point in the shape of a single flame.

The three at the front abruptly came to a standstill and turned to face one another, forming an aisle in between. In the space they created stood Criada. There were two guards stood in the middle with her, each holding into an arm. The head maid, now a prisoner, had her hands bound by rope. Criada stood crossly, still trying to tug away from the guards' grasp, glaring at all she could see.

"We are gathered here today, to mark an end to these dark times." The strong, booming voice came from King Karalius. Lottie and the others immediately looked back to the king, bowing their heads a little as he spoke. His stern gaze darted around the chamber defiantly. Lottie thought King Karalius looked ready to behead anyone who dared interrupt him. No wonder, she thought, given everything that had happened. King Karalius fixed his glare onto his former servant.

"Criada, you have committed treason." The king's voice was icy, but far calmer than Lottie had expected. Lottie glanced to Criada and almost gasped. She looked nothing like the calm, mild-mannered woman Lottie had first met yesterday morning. Lottie realised now that the kindness had probably never been there at all.

Criada now looked manic and panicked, yet she held the king's gaze defiantly. There didn't seem to be a single shred of remorse in her features. Criada was yet to stand still. Instead, the gold freckles upon the deep blue of her arms were dancing wildly, as she tried desperately to break free. Despite the blue and gold sparkling in the sunlight pouring through the crystal windows, her movements were anything but beautiful. Rather Criada's skin looked just as mad as she did herself, as if her skin was trying to break free, too.

"What say you?" King Karalius suddenly roared. At his fiery question, Criada immediately stopped squirming, still glaring at her king. The former maid twisted her mouth up into a sneer, crueller than Lottie had ever seen before.

"You'll never know where the locket is, my liege," Criada answered him sarcastically. With a jolt to her heart, Lottie realised Criada still thought her locket was hidden. She was wearing it now, but her pendant was tucked underneath her clothes. Criada was obviously just hoping Lottie and the others hadn't worked it out; that the locket was still hidden, wrapped in a cloth in the stables.

"Soon, its mysteries will be unleashed and the power within it will be harnessed. Not only will the human girl be stuck here…" Criada's voice faded, as her eyes flickered to Lottie, the sneer growing. Lottie took a small step back, filled with horror. She knew then she would never forget that terrifying expression, for as long as she lived. Yet there was another part of her that wanted to defy this horrible woman. She was looking forward to revealing that she was wearing her locket.

"War itself will soon rage across Orovand," Criada resumed, her gaze reverting to the king's. "Orovand has been ruled by its corrupt cities for long enough, especially Oruvesi," she spat the words. "You may kill me, sire," she added sarcastically, "but your reign will end soon—"

"Silence!" King Karalius roared, far angrier than anybody

Lottie had ever seen before. "I will not tolerate such wicked speech! Your treason is far worse than I ever imagined," he snarled.

"Do you think you are invisible?" she continued softly. "That you have not made any mistakes? That you could never be harmed, my king?" Her words were deathly soft, a clear threat laced across her speech. As terrifying as King Karalius' roars in anger were, Lottie knew that Criada's wicked whispers were far more dangerous and deadly.

"We have planned this for years, my king, yet you never saw it!" Criada declared triumphantly, her voice much more like normal. A smug grin crossed her face. "It was perfect."

"Oh really?" The daring challenge in King Karalius' voice, almost as soft as Criada's had been, abruptly changed Criada's face. The ghost of the grin was still there, but Lottie saw something else lurking in her eyes now. Was it fear? "We'll see about that, shall we?" the king scorned.

"You know nothing," Criada hissed, but her flickering eyes betrayed that she was not at all sure the king was bluffing.

"No, Criada," King Karalius replied, speaking slowly and softly. "It is you who know nothing. For this human child you speak of, this wonderful girl who is the daughter of Julie Sawyer, has solved these dreadful mysteries for us." King Karalius glanced to Lottie.

"Show her," King Karalius nodded to her. The king's gaze was suddenly kind, as it had been at their first meeting two days ago, in this very chamber. Unlike the scornful, hateful eyes of Criada, Lottie knew she could place all her trust in the king's gentle gaze.

"Your Majesty," Lottie responded, stepping forwards as the moment came to silence Criada once and for all. With a single flourish of her hand, Lottie plucked the locket from underneath her top, brandishing it for the former maid to see.

"No!" Criada shouted, squirming again against her captors, eyes wide with hate. "How could you... how did you?" She was so filled with angry despair, she couldn't even finish her sentences.

"You were the one who made mistakes, Criada," Lottie said, amazed at how calm her voice was. "If you thought the locket was unsafe under the floorboards, then you shouldn't have left your muddy boots there," she pointed out.

"Lottie figured it out," Andri chimed in smugly, folding his arms. Lottie realised he was speaking without permission, but she reasoned he probably could, being the prince. "She worked it out last night that you must have made all that stuff up, about hearing a strange noise. There couldn't have been an intruder, because you were the only thief. You got your boots muddy in the stables, when you hid the locket in there," Andri concluded.

"You must have just panicked, seeing that all the other boots were clean," Lottie then resumed. "Your muddy ones might have even been traced back to you. So, you hid them in the only place you knew—under the loose floorboards in your room."

"You had no idea Dendari would drop the note you gave him, though did you? Which led us to your muddy boots that eventually led us to your locket," Andri challenged.

"Dendari was a fool," Criada spat, starting to wrestle again against her restraints. "We would have done it all, if it wasn't for him."

"The clumsiness of the baker is most fortunate," King Karalius agreed, smiling darkly. "Which leads us to the next question… where is Dendari?" He roared. Criada became still but said nothing.

"If tell me," he said his voice suddenly much quieter, "then perhaps I will grant you some small, measure of mercy. It is over, Criada. I will spare your life, if you reveal the missing secrets. Otherwise, I will slay you where you stand." The king motioned one of the palace guard to bring his sword, large and gold and embedded with red jewels. Lottie gasped. Would he really kill her here?

"Very well, Your Majesty," Criada rasped, as the two captors forced her to walk forwards toward the king. "I shall tell you what you seek." King Karalius raised his hand, his other now clenched around the jewel-encrusted hilt of his sword, a little drawn from the sheath at his belt.

"You should ask Opin, since he is Dendari's brother," the maid declared turning to glare at the official.

"No!" Opin groaned. Everyone else collectively gasped, horrified. Even the king, normally stood so stoically, had his mouth hanging open at the shocking revelation. "Criada, how could you?"

"His Majesty promised me my life," Criada replied, then sneered at him. "Or were you never going to tell us that the official from Tilajin is also from the Mavi Mountains? What I speak of is the truth, Your Majesty," Criada returned, turning back to the king. "Opin, Dendari and I were going to leave tonight, once I had retrieved the locket from the stables. Dendari is still here, Your Majesty, in the palace," Criada revealed. "He is hiding in Opin's wardrobe."

"Seize him!" King Karalius bellowed, pointing at Opin. The three palace guards who'd been standing in front of Criada grabbed hold of him, before Opin could take a single step.

King Karalius sat down on his throne again, one hand still holding his sword. "Go to Opin's chamber and retrieve that murderous baker, right this moment!" he shouted. The king's free hand slapped against one of the arms of the throne as he spoke.

As the three guards standing behind Criada darted from the room, the rest of them stayed in a state of shocked, uneasy silence. Lottie felt numb. Opin was Dendari's brother? Opin, Criada and Dendari had been working together, all this time? Dendari had somehow snuck back to the palace after being dropped off at the inn and was hiding in Opin's wardrobe? It was such a lot to take in.

"No doubt you wanted to escape as soon as Criada was captured," King Karalius growled to Opin, while they waited for the guards to bring Dendari to the throne room. The official from Tilajin raised his head from where he'd been stood staring at the floor, unable to look his king in the eye. "Except that I had guards following your every move, did I not?"

"Yes, Your Majesty," Opin replied heavily, sounding hollow. "I knew it would be unsafe to move my brother. I had to hope Criada would keep her mouth shut... but she did not."

"At last!" King Karalius roared, standing again as Dendari was pushed into the room. The king drew his sword, brandishing it towards Dendari. Lottie bit her lip, feeling a bit sick. She wondered if she might faint, or maybe throw up, if the king killed the baker here and now.

As they spoke, Lottie couldn't take her eyes off Dendari. Where was the kind baker who had given her the cronzaki to welcome her to Orovand? She had not seen him since meeting him in the square that first evening. The man was transformed, an angry glare upon his face, as he twisted in his chains like

Criada was still doing. Watching him, Lottie was reminded of a wounded animal. He seemed defeated, but with strength enough to break free and bite every single one of them if they let him.

"Lord Jakad's death was necessary," Dendari spoke, his voice rough and angry, nothing like the warming, gentle tones Lottie had first heard. He was also speaking without permission, but she supposed the king would have hardly noticed this, given the baker's far greater crime. "Lord Jakad was weak," Dendari was saying. "The perfect pawn that we could use to start war across Orovand. Since you banished us from the mountains, you have decreed the rest of the Mavi people to poverty. It was worth it, if only to wipe your pompous smirk—"

"Enough!" King Karalius bellowed. Dendari fell into silence, still glaring. "Guira said they had followed you to an inn, far to the south side of Oruvesi. Why did you return?" the king demanded.

"I spent yesterday walking back to the palace," Dendari admitted. "I realised when I was dressing that morning in the inn that I'd dropped the note from Criada in Karoc's carriage. I walked back to retrieve the note, but when I got to the palace, Opin told me it had already been found and Criada was captured. Then, we found out the girl had got back to the palace, having found the salt in my stall, so I had no choice but to hide."

"You're a fool, Dendari," Criada spat again. "We could've succeeded if only you hadn't dropped my note. You have doomed us all!" she ended in a shout.

"Silence," King Karalius ordered, his voice only a little louder. "Out of respect for the children present, you will not receive the punishment for your treason here, baker," the king added. Lottie tried not to flinch. She was glad she wouldn't have to witness anything horrible. She didn't want to imagine the horrors that could be in store for Dendari. "I will decide upon your fate later, Criada," the king snarled, looking to the thief.

"Opin, you will also face a punishment fitting for your crime." King Karalius glared at the official from Tilajin. Opin could only bear to hold his king's gaze for a moment, before he lowered his head again. "You may not have stolen Lottie's locket, or poisoned Lord Jakad, but you have harboured a criminal," he said.

"Before you depart, I shall make one thing abundantly clear," the king said, brandishing his sword towards all three of them. "It is tragic what happened to your town, but I acted on the wisdom of those who tested the Mavi Mountains and found them unsafe. You can examine the records if you wish, which showed an increased rate of rocks falling. Once the town was deemed unsafe, Oruvesi and the other cities welcomed the people from the mountains in. We gave your people the chance to start a new life," he concluded.

"Not a single rock has fallen near enough to the town to make it dangerous," Dendari disagreed sharply, looking up to the king he had betrayed.

"You are entitled to your opinion, if you feel you have been treated unjustly," King Karalius returned, then glared. "Your views do not, however, give you liberty to steal and murder, to attempt to start a war, merely to get revenge. Take them to the dungeons!" The king roared. There was a moment's silence before the palace guards marched back out, this time taking Dendari and Opin into custody as well as

Criada.

"I hope for your sake, you have not been involved, Uradna," King Karalius added, turning his gaze upon the official from Edowoda. "You will go to your chamber and remain there."

"Your Majesty," Uradna replied to his stern order, bowing as a tear formed in her eye. "I assure you, my king, I had no idea. I have always been faithful." The rest of them watched as she retreated, the double-doors swinging shut behind her.

"Such dreadful events," King Karalius muttered mournfully, descending the palace steps as the traitors were led away. As the king replaced his sword with a definitive clink, Lottie took a deep breath, then slowly let it all out again. It was finally over, with Criada's shocking confession that not only was Dendari the murderer, but also Opin's brother.

"Lottie, I have to thank you," King Karalius said now, extending his hand to her. Lottie bowed her head, as he touched her shoulder briefly. Lottie was still a little fearful of the king, but his wrath seemed to have disappeared as quickly as it had arisen. She realised that even if he wasn't always the gentlest king, he was always a good king, one his people could trust.

"All of you," the king said, looking around his throne room as he spoke, then glancing to to Andri, Guira and Zara. "In solving this mystery, you have saved all of Orovand from war." The king smiled, looking totally different to his angry glare.

"If I might, Your Majesty." The deep voice came from Preto, who stepped forward and bowed low as he spoke. King Karalius nodded, gesturing his hand to let the Guardian of the Lockets speak. "Lottie, may I see your locket?" Lottie nodded, reaching up to unclasp it.

"It is as I thought," Preto said regretfully, as he held it up to his face. "I had a theory that the power of the locket may fade faster, the longer it was separated from you. There is far less of the gold energy than I thought."

"Am I too late?" Lottie gasped, her eyes filling with fear at the prospect of spending a year in Orovand. "I wasn't sure if Criada could have tampered with it or something last night."

At least it was a year, in the Gold Dimension's time, she tried to encourage herself, as Preto continued to study her locket. That hopefully only meant a few months in Earth's time. That was much shorter than forever.

"I don't think so," Preto concluded, after surveying the locket, giving her a small smile. "The locket looks perfectly safe to me. There seems to be enough power left, for now. With your permission, Your Majesty, we must hurry."

"Of course. We will all accompany you," King Karalius signalled to a palace guard. "Carriages at once," he added simply. With that, Lottie suddenly was leaving the throne room for the last time, as they hurried her down from the throne room and out of the main hall. They only paused whilst Lottie and Guira rushed back into her spare bedroom for Lottie to change back into the pyjamas, fluffy dressing gown and fluffy socks she had arrived in two days' previously.

As they sped back to the entrance hall, Lottie bit her lip trying to make sense of her warring emotions. A few minutes ago, she wasn't even sure where Dendari was. In her heart, she had hoped to spend the rest of the day with Zara and Andri, to relax a bit and enjoy some more time with them before saying a proper goodbye. Now it looked like they wouldn't have that chance. Now she had her locket back, Orovand had abruptly gone back to a paradise again. Lottie realised she wasn't quite ready to leave the Gold Dimension yet.

"It'll be all right, Lottie," Guira offered kindly, as they stepped once more into the carriage. Zara's mother put her arm around her, as the carriage gently began rocking them away. Lottie stared out of the window, keeping her gaze on the palace and the beautiful, golden buildings of Oruvesi, sparkling and shimmering in the sunshine, until they faded from view.

"I…" Lottie hardly knew where to begin, as tears threatened to form. Did she really have to give up the friends she'd just made, her only friends in the world? In lots of ways, Lottie felt like she had belonged more in the Gold Dimension than she ever had on Earth. Would she now have to go back?

"I know it's hard, Lottie," Zara said, reaching out to grab her friend's hands. "but this is a good thing." Zara spoke with tears in her eyes, so suddenly Lottie wasn't so sure. "You'll see your home again, Lottie, all your friends." Lottie bit her lip harder, as tears threatened to fall.

"That's just it, though," Lottie muttered, squeezing Zara's hands back. "I don't have any proper friends back home, really. Not like you and Andri," she burst out.

"Think of all you've accomplished, Lottie," Andri replied, a single tremor of emotion in his voice. He sat forward a little in his seat. "You've solved a murder and a theft, all in two days! Stopping a war from starting in our lands while you're at it, too! You're so much stronger than you know, Lottie," the Prince of Orovand emphasised. "Think of how much you can achieve back home now. You just need to be yourself."

"I had a lot of help, though," Lottie pointed out, glancing between Andri and Zara. "I couldn't have done it without you, both of you." She tried not to cry. "You... you're my best friends."

"You're my best friend too, Lottie," Zara muttered, the first few tears spilling from her eyes. "I'm sure going to miss you."

"We all will," Guira added, smiling as they entered the turquoise wood. "Zara said you'll start a new school soon. You should excel in that, given all you've done here in just one day. I hope everyone you know on Earth will see you for you who you are," Guira spoke a little roughly. "for I'm not sure I know anyone as kind, as brave, or as clever."

"Yeah, or they'll have us to answer to, won't they?" Andri gently teased. A smile twitched gently at Lottie' lips as she swiped at her eyes, at last starting to believe in all the positive things they were saying.

Maybe school wouldn't be as hard as she'd thought, Lottie thought to herself. Maybe she'd find making friends a little easier, because it had to be easier than solving a murder case and stopping a war. Also, Lottie reflected, as the carriage took them along the path through the wood, she had learnt an important lesson while she was here.

Maybe, it was okay to be who she was, to accept that she was quiet and a bit anxious. Perhaps there wasn't necessarily anything wrong with that, so maybe she didn't have to keep beating herself up about it. Perhaps, it was simply part of herself, just like Zara not being able to sit still or being a bit loud was part of who she was. Maybe, Lottie thought, everybody had different strengths and weaknesses, because people were different. Perhaps that was fine, even good.

"We're here," Andri announced, as the carriage came to a stop. King Karalius had taken a second carriage with Preto and the six of them hurried into the cave.

"Looks like we are just in time," Preto murmured, glancing to Lottie's locket again. "I'll start the ceremony." He almost ran to the pedestal, placing his sword down upon it.

"Orovand owes you a great debt, Lottie Armitage," King Karalius declared, stepping forward to take her hands again. "We will sing your praises, just as we sang the praises of your mother."

"Thank you, Your Majesty," Lottie answered him only a little shakily, before shifting her gaze to Guira, Zara and Andri.

"It's been so wonderful to meet all of you," Lottie muttered, tears threatening to obscure her vision as she approached her friends. "Thank you so much," she murmured, hugging Guira first. "Your Highness," she added, her tone gently teasing to Andri as she turned to the prince. His smile broadened, as the two of them shared a quick hug.

"Zara," Lottie muttered, turning to Guira's daughter, the girl Lottie knew was her best friend. Maybe she always would be, even if she was from another realm. Even if they never met again.

"It's been amazing, Lottie," Zara managed, as the two friends hugged each other hard. Lottie felt her tears flow faster as she embraced Zara tightly, this girl who she loved as much as a sister.

"Sorry, Miss Lottie, but I am ready," Preto apologised. "We must act now if you are to return safely." Slowly, Lottie disengaged herself from Zara.

"It's all right," Lottie murmured, managing to give Preto a small smile. "Thank you," she said to the Locket Guardian, who bowed his head in response. Lottie slid into the gold water, cool but not cold to the touch.

"You will wake up at home, Lottie," Preto instructed. "If you're ready," he added. Lottie nodded, her throat too tight to speak as she looked back again to Andri, Zara, Guira and the king.

"Farewell, Lottie Armitage, daughter of Julie Sawyer," King Karalius spoke, gesturing grandly. Lottie managed to smile again, despite the tears that were mixing with the golden water.

"Goodbye everyone. Thank you all," Lottie replied hurriedly. At Preto's nod, Lottie closed her eyes, breathing deeply. Her locket began to glow. Lottie felt a bit hot and faint again, just like last time. Quickly, Lottie took a deep breath and ducked her head under the cool golden water. There was an almost blinding flash of light, then a crackling sound like a whip. Just like that, Lottie had left the Gold Dimension.

Chapter Sixteen

Lottie's eyes snapped open, panting and gasping for breath as adrenaline surged through her. She blinked, looking around. She was back in the spare bedroom in Aunt Susan's creepy old barn in rural Yorkshire. It had worked—she was back on Earth. The filtering light through the curtains told her it was day. Lottie sighed, resting back against the headboard of the bed. She was pleasantly surprised at how content she was to be back, despite leaving her friends in Orovand.

Lottie had a sudden urge to leap out of bed, go to her aunt's room and give her a massive hug, but as her feet touched the floor, she paused. How long had she been gone? She knew that time passed differently in the Gold Dimension. Had Aunt Susan even realised she was gone? Lottie shifted back on the bed, her glance falling to the alarm clock on her bedside table.

It was 12pm. Lottie shook her head, for it boggled her mind and was too much for her to process. She had sent the equivalent of a weekend in the Gold Dimension, forty hours or so, only to have twelve hours or so pass on Earth. She blinked, beginning to feel light-headed and suddenly exhausted. No wonder, given all that she'd done in the space of half a day back home.

"Lottie? Please come out, wherever you are. Are you hiding?" Aunt Susan asked, exasperated. Lottie heard that her voice was near. Her eyes widened in alarm. Susan had obviously come upstairs to find her missing.

"I'm here, Aunt," Lottie called down immediately, before she'd even worked out what she was going to say. She had no idea how she would explain her absence, but the first thing to do was to stop Susan getting so worried she called the police or something.

"Oh, thank goodness!" Lottie heard her aunt running upstairs. She leapt out of bed, tightening her dressing gown. She'd just slipped her locket underneath her pyjama top when the bedroom door opened.

"There you are! Where have you been?" Aunt Susan's anxious face came into view. "Have... have you only just gotten up?" Her aunt's face creased in confusion. "I came up here about an hour ago, you weren't here."

"I was just opening my presents," Lottie explained, gesturing the discarded glittery wrapper that the jewellery box had been wrapped in. Technically this was true, as it was the last thing Lottie did before going to the Gold Dimension. Seeing Susan's confusion and suspicion, Lottie had no choice but to plough on with her deception. How else would she explain it?

"I, uh, was a bit bored after opening my presents," she explained next. "Your house is just as big as I remember it when I was little, so I decided to do a bit of exploring. I guess when I was wandering around, I didn't hear you calling," Lottie added with a shrug. "I've only just come back to my room. "Sorry if I worried you, Auntie."

"Well, you're here and safe, I guess that's the important thing," Susan added. Her expression cleared and Lottie let out the breath she didn't realise she'd been holding.

"Well, anyway, happy birthday, Lottie!" Susan declared

with a grin. "Why don't you get dressed and I'll get you some lunch. We still have lots of your birthday left to celebrate!"

"Thanks, Auntie, sorry again," Lottie smiled. Susan left the room and Lottie sat down on her bed, thankful Susan had decided to believe her. In the clear light of day on Earth, Lottie frowned. Had it all been a dream? she wondered. She closed her eyes briefly, thinking of Orovand, where everything was flecked with gold, with mountains of deep blue and turquoise trees and grass.

No, Lottie thought, reaching into her dressing gown pocket. She brought out the distinctive wrapping paper, from the cronzaki Dendari had given her on her first day in Orovand. Unfortunately, the girl could never think about the heavenly snack again in the same way, without thinking of how the baker had attempted treason, but the wrapper proved the events of this weekend were real. Lottie stood then, to get dressed and headed downstairs.

"Happy birthday to you…" as Lottie headed downstairs, she heard the slightly cat-strangling sound of her aunt singing. "Happy birthday to you…" Lottie frowned. The inharmonious noise was not really helping her headache very much at all. "Happy birthday, dear Lottie…" Lottie walked into the kitchen, "happy birthday to you!" Aunt Susan handed her niece a mug of tea, grinning broadly. Lottie had never been so happy to hear a song finishing, even if it was for her.

"Thanks, Auntie," Lottie said and smiled, accepting the mug. Lottie blew on the hot tea and took a strong, comforting sip.

"What's that you're wearing?" Aunt Susan asked, nodding to Lottie. "Was it a birthday present?" With some alarm, Lottie realised her locket had slipped back out of her pyjama top.

"Yes, um… I woke up around midnight and couldn't get back to sleep, so I opened it then," Lottie admitted honestly. "It's this locket," Lottie said, seeing there was no other way around it. Besides, maybe she was just being paranoid. She was sure Aunt Susan would never steal it, nor think there was anything extraordinary about it. Lottie handed her mug back to Susan for a moment, so she could unclasp it. "I think I fell asleep wearing it."

"That locket belonged to Julie," Susan murmured. "May I?" At Lottie's nod, Susan reached for the pendant, roving her finger over the gold surface with its mysterious etchings. "Julie got it for her eleventh birthday too," Susan added with a smile. "It's been in our family for generations. Apparently, an ancestor bought it, hundreds of years ago, from an artisan's stall." Aunt Susan gave a thoughtful frown as she peered at the locket.

Lottie's eyes widened slightly as she listened—that certainly fit the theory that all the humans who had visited Orovand came from the same bloodline, which was how they were able to get there.

"Not long after your mum got it, she began making up stories," her aunt continued, "She would tell me about how the locket would take her to a brand-new world. Maybe it will give you new adventures, too, if you're not that old for that sort of thing," Aunt Susan quipped.

"Maybe," was Lottie's only reply, with a smile back. She took another mouthful of tea, now cool enough to drink. As Lottie went for another gulp, the doorbell sounded.

"Ah, just in time for your birthday surprise," Aunt Susan smiled with a wink. Lottie frowned in confusion up at her aunt.

"Shall we see who's at the door?" Her aunt left the kitchen, leaving Lottie to follow, wondering who the surprise visitors might be.

"Mum!" Lottie gasped with excitement to see her mother standing in the doorway. Behind her was her father. "Dad!" Lottie was hardly aware of her feet moving as she dove into the embrace of Julie Armitage.

"Surprise!" her mother said, cracking a grin as, her arms naturally fell around Lottie. The girl hugged her mother hard. "Happy birthday, Lottie," Julie muttered, moving to kiss the top of her daughter's head. "You okay?" she asked softly, when Lottie still didn't let go. She felt tears begin to prick at the back of her eyes.

"Yeah, I'm fine," Lottie said, a little too brightly and a little too quickly. Then she grinned. "I was just surprised, that's all."

"Well, that was kind of the idea, poppet," Malcolm Armitage winked. "Nadia suddenly got a job interview she needed to prep for. We knew we'd just be in the way, so we thought we'd get away early and surprise you."

"That's so lovely," Lottie beamed. "Is Nadia okay?" she added, sobering a little as she looked between her parents. "I'm sorry I was so grumpy about you going. I want her to be happy," she said definitively. The trip to the Gold Dimension had certainly given her some perspective about what really mattered. Her sister's happiness was one of those things, even if she wasn't in touch with Nadia much.

"That's really kind and grown-up of you, Lottie," her dad commented. "Yeah, she's okay. She's broken up with Sean… it's for the best," he clarified with certainty. Lottie had only met Sean once, but her father had developed a less than radiant view of him very quickly. "We helped her move in with a friend. She sends you love, kiddo. So," he said, as the three of them traipsed into the living room. "Did you have any adventures while you've been here?"

"Of course, Dad," Lottie joked then her gaze found her mother and stayed. "There's lots of adventures to be had in rural Yorkshire. Thanks so much for the locket, Mum," she added, as deliberately as he could.

"You're very welcome, love," Julie replied. There was a knowing look in her eyes. "You want to help me make some tea for everyone?" she added.

"Absolutely," Lottie said at once. The two of them went straight for the kitchen. As she left, she heard her dad joke that he'd never heard anyone be so enthusiastic about making tea.

"Well?" Julie asked quietly, going straight to the point as Lottie shut the door behind them. Julie clicked the kettle on and turned back to her daughter. "Did you...?"

"I've been there," Lottie said, nodding. "I've been to Orovand." Julie grinned, smiling in delight as she leant against the kitchen sink, waiting. "It's the most beautiful place I've ever seen," Lottie whispered. "I'll never forget it, not if I live to be five hundred. Thank you so much."

"You're welcome, Lottie. I knew you'd love it. I thought about telling you more, in the note. I thought about warning you for what you were in for, but... you'd never have believed me," her mum shrugged, as the kettle began to chug and gurgle, nearly reaching boiling point.

"I know," Lottie agreed, reaching for mugs. "Some things have to be lived, rather than told," she said to her mother, popping the tea bags into the pot. Julie smiled and nodded. "That's why you gave me so many swimming lessons, isn't it?

231

You knew one day I might need it."

"Yes, that's right. I think your dad wondered why I wanted you to swim so much when you were little, rather than focus on another sport. He doesn't know," she added definitively. "Nobody else knows. Nobody would've believed me," she repeated.

"I understand," Lottie replied solemnly, as her mother poured the boiling water into the pot. "There is one thing I don't get, Mum," she sad now. "Why give the locket to me? Nadia is older, shouldn't she have inherited it?" Julie smiled as she replaced the kettle onto the stand.

"Well, it's because the locket chose you," Julie replied with a smile, reaching out to stroke a strand of her daughter's hair away from her face. "You know what I mean about the locket calling to you?" she asked quietly. Lottie nodded, understanding at once, for she too had heard the locket resonating deeply with her own soul.

"After Nadia was born, I put the locket near her, but nothing happened. I didn't feel anything from the locket," her mother explained. "I started to wonder if it would work at all, but then I had you. When I put the locket near you, Lottie— oh, I felt something." A single tear trailed down her mother's face as she smiled. "The calling was even louder than when I went to Orovand myself. I knew then that the locket should go to you, rather than Nadia. It was like instinct, like I understood exactly what the locket was saying." Julie swished the teabags around in the pot as she talked.

"I'm so happy it came to you, as well," her mum said, "I think... Nadia's always been so loud, so confident... bossy at times," Julie admitted with a smile. "Whereas you're quieter, you've maybe found things a bit harder. I feel like maybe you needed the adventure to Orovand, more than she did." She paused in the swirling of her teabags to glance to her daughter. "Am I wrong?"

"No," Lottie replied immediately. "You're not wrong. This is… one of the best things that's ever happened to me." Julie smiled broadly at this. "They remember you, Mum; you're a legend. Everyone kept saying how I was your daughter."

"That's nice, if not a little strange. Probably you will be too," Julie agreed, beginning to pour the tea into the mugs. "A long time will have passed for Orovand."

"A hundred years since your thirty years on Earth," Lottie nodded in agreement. "I was there about forty hours, but twelve hours passed on Earth," she calculated.

Quickly, Lottie then told her mum everything that happened in Orovand. Julie listened with wide eyes, as Lottie talked about meeting Guira, Zara and Andri, about meeting King Karalius and the ceremony. Lottie spoke even faster, then, telling her mother about solving the case of her locket being stolen and Lord Jakad's murder, just in time to travel back to Earth.

"How's it going?" Lottie finished abruptly as her father entered the kitchen. "You two have been ages. Having a nice chat?" he said kindly, ruffling Lottie's hair. "I just wanted to remind you that Susan takes one sugar," he told his wife. "Can you help me with the mugs, kiddo?"

"Uh, sure," Lottie answered, smiling at her mother knowingly; happy it was their secret. Lottie grabbed two mugs and took them back through to the living room.

"Happy birthday to you…" Lottie's eyes widened as Susan, with her sadly terrible singing, brought a cake into the room. It had eleven candles and a number eleven out of the small, metallic letters one buys for these things. Lottie grinned, beaming with excitement.

"I haven't had breakfast yet!" Was all she could think of to say. Everyone began laughing. "I had a bit of a lie in," Lottie grinned.

"That's a bit of an understatement. I was a bit worried; I thought Lottie had disappeared on me." she added, a hint of a rebuke in her tone that reminded Lottie very much of Guira, "because she wasn't in her bedroom. She decided to do some exploring."

"Trying to find an adventure after all, were you, kiddo?" Lottie's dad gently teased, while her mum stayed quiet with just the glimmer of a secret in her eyes. Lottie knew that her mum would've worked out that just half an hour or so before, Lottie was still in the Gold Dimension.

"Well, just this once, maybe you can have cake for your breakfast," her dad said, then grinned as Susan began cutting up the cake and passing it round. "After all, you only turn eleven once," her dad said affectionately. Lottie grinned, realising the irony of his words.

For in her adventure of a lifetime of going to Orovand, she had already had one birthday. As she tucked into her cake, Lottie realised that with going to the Gold Dimension and back again, she had turned eleven twice. Lottie knew she would never forget her birthday adventure to Orovand, not for as long as she lived.